UNSAID THINGS

Stories by

Joanna Acevedo

Flexible Press
Minneapolis, Minnesota 2021

Print ISBN: 978-1-7364033-0-3
eBook ISBN: 978-1-7364033-1-0

Flexible Press LLC

Editor William E Burleson

Copy editor Vicki Adang,
Mark My Words Editorial Services, LLC

Cover art via Canva.com

The story "Pursuit" previously appeared in
Bridge: The Bluffton University Literary Journal

What people are saying:

"Blunt, spare, tautly-honed stories in which lovers wound each other, betray and abandon each other, return to each other, fall in love, out of love, and back in love again, in a Mobius strip of hard-edged prose that captures the unsentimental sexual politics of our time. Joanna Acevedo is an unflinching portraitist with a wicked sense of humor." —Joyce Carol Oates, winner of the PEN/O. Henry Award, the National Book Award, and the National Book Critics' Circle Award.

"Joanna Acevedo has many gifts, but the most potent may be: she is a writer who is incapable of being dull. This searing, mesmerizingly entertaining collection will leave you aching for more. She's a great writer, and this is an exhilarating debut."—Darin Strauss, author of numerous books including *Half a Life* and recipient of the National Book Critics Circle Award.

"I wish I could read Joanna Acevedo for the first time again, and feel that swell of amazement a reader feels when discovering a brave and brilliant writer and thinker ... I envy you, reader, encountering Joanna Acevedo at the beginning of a great career." — Sharon Mesmer, poet, fiction writer, essayist and professor of creative writing.

"Love isn't safe, love isn't kind. Love is a four letter word in Joanna Acevedo's *Unsaid Things*."—Elisa Sinnett, author of *Detroit Fairy Tales*.

Dedicated to all the men
I've loved and lost.

Contents

Loss Can Be Gradual or All at Once

Alex has a smoke stain on his two front teeth, and he is leaving. "Don't," I say. He doesn't listen. He is packing up his suitcase, and he is going, going, gone. Loss can be gradual or all at once.

When he left me the first time, I told people he was dead. I told them there had been a tragic accident. "How quaint," they all said, as if people don't die anymore. We had mutual friends. It got awkward. People started seeing him in restaurants and saying, "Shandy told me you were dead." It took about three months, but eventually he called me.

"You've been telling people I'm dead," he said when I picked up the phone, trying not to be excited that he called. I was painting my toenails. He had given me the apartment, moved all his stuff out in the middle of the night, and told me not to call him anymore.

"What?" I said. "No, I haven't."

"Yes, you have," he said. "Like, four people have asked me why I'm not dead. And they all say the rumor came from you."

"Why would I tell people you were dead?" I said, even though there was a host of perfectly good reasons. "That doesn't make any sense."

"I don't know *why* you would tell people I was dead," he said. "I just know that you're doing it. And I'm calling to ask you, as a friend, to stop."

"We're not friends," I said. "You made that perfectly clear when you told me not to call you anymore."

"Well, then I'm not asking as a friend," he said. "As another human being, I'm asking you to please stop telling people that I'm dead. Since I'm clearly not. Dead, that is."

"I would stop," I said, hoping for plausible deniability, "but as I haven't been doing that, I won't stop doing anything."

Alex sighed. I could hear him smoking a cigarette over the phone. I listened to him breathe. "Shandy," he said. "Don't be an asshole."

"Sure, Alex," I said. "Look, why don't you buy me dinner, and we can talk about it."

He exhaled. I knew I had him.

Now he's leaving again. This time we lasted two months. Before that, six months. Before that, three months. After a certain point, Alex decides he can't take it anymore, and he leaves. But he always comes back.

*

When he left me the second time, I told people he had gone to fat camp. "But he's not fat," people said.

"You must not have seen him in a while," I said. "He was getting pretty hefty. You know how it is, when you're on a deadline, and all you do is eat takeout and don't exercise. I still love him though."

"That's so good of you," people said.

"It really is," I said.

After a certain point, though, people started seeing Alex around, and they could tell he wasn't fat. And then he called me.

"I don't even think adults can go to fat camp," he said on the phone. "I think that's like, the *Biggest Loser* or something. Obviously I'm not at fat camp."

"I don't know where you heard that," I said. "That's so coincidental. Wow."

"Shandy," he said. "I just need you to stop telling people lies about me. And maybe, I don't know, get some professional help."

"Why would I need professional help?" I said.

"Because you keep doing this," he said. "I'm getting really tired of making these phone calls, you know."

"Then stop calling me," I said, even though I wanted nothing less. "You're the one picking up the phone, not me."

"You called me fourteen times yesterday," he said.

"No, I didn't," I said. "Honestly, you should get your phone checked. Or maybe," I said, "you should get some professional help. You seem to be having a lot of delusions lately. Anyway," I finished, "what are you up to tonight?"

Alex throws some clothes into a duffel bag. "This time," he says, "I mean it. I'm done."

"You always say that," I say.

"Well, this time I'm really saying it."

"Oh, come on."

"And don't even think about trying to make up some lie to get me back," he says. "I'm not falling for that again."

He's fallen for it three times now. I turn up my nose.

"Sure," I say. "Of course."

The last time Alex left me, I told people he had won a fellowship in another state. "Oh, wow," they said. "That's so good for him. He'll really get a lot of work done."

Alex called me after two weeks this time. He had run into one of our friends and they had said, "I thought you were out of town."

"I don't know why you do these things," he said to me. "I don't know what's wrong with you."

"Me either," I said. "But I wish it was something else."

"What am I supposed to do?" he asked me. "What do you want me to do?"

"Come over," I said. "I'm making pot roast."

*

Alex says we can go out on the fire escape and smoke a cigarette. "I just don't think you're good for me," he says. "That's not a judgment on you. I just don't think I can do my best work when you're around."

"I thought you said I was your muse," I say.

"That was then," he says. "I'm working on a new project now."

"Is there someone else?" I say.

"No," he says. "But if there was, I wouldn't tell you."

Alex and I met at a party about a year ago. I was telling people I was a famous actress from L.A., and Alex was telling people he was a famous artist. One of us was lying.

He spotted me from across the room. That's what he always says, anyway. I told him my name was Matilda and I was originally from Germany.

"You have almost no accent," he said.

"Thank you."

Alex was from Brooklyn. He had a show in Chelsea, photography, but he didn't call himself a photographer. He had a girlfriend who lived in Queens and laughingly said they were in a long-distance relationship. We had sex in the single bathroom in the apartment while a line formed outside.

"Do you want to move into my apartment?" I asked when he was finished.

"Where do you live?" he asked.

"Bushwick."

"Sure," he said.

"One more thing," I said. "I have cats."

"How many cats?" he said.

When Alex leaves, I look at the cat winding herself around my legs. The apartment feels empty without him. He has taken his clothes from the dresser, his shoes from the hall. Probably he's gone back to the ex-girlfriend in Queens.

I go to the fridge and take out a frozen burrito and stick it in the microwave. Then I call my friend, Michele. Bending down to pet the cat, I wait for my burrito to heat up. Michele picks up the phone.

"Shandy," she says. "What's up?"

"You're never going to believe what Alex did this time," I say.

"Oh my God," she says. "I can't wait to hear."

Visiting Hours

Mac was sixteen and a son of a bitch, and I loved him the way you love the sun, in that you're grateful for its warmth but you don't look at it for too long because you'll burn out your retinas. I would have done anything for him, but I wouldn't have ever said it out loud because he would have taken that knowledge and done something horrible with it. The way that Mac showed you he cared was to be cruel. Cruelty is a sort of kindness—that's what he always said—because at least cruelty is honest. Mac liked honesty.

We were friends because he was the only other kid on the block. Our neighborhood was mostly childless couples and old people. Mac was a delinquent and a truant, and I wasn't much better. Half the time he didn't bother to go to school, wandering around the developments doing God knows what with the boys from the other side of town. When he went to school, he cut class and passed notes and stole library books, and he was in detention all the time. I would wait in the parking lot for him, scuffing my shoe against the pavement, until he was finally let free.

For a while, we did nothing but steal mailboxes, until there were none left on the whole street. Once Mac coerced the neighbor's cat to follow him up into the treehouse, where he was going to do something awful, but I convinced him not to; we fed it scraps of a turkey sandwich instead. Eventually it was so tame that it followed us around everywhere, completely abandoning its owner. When the cat died last year, we gave him a Viking funeral in the reservoir. Mac filled the boat with firecrackers bought across the Penn-Jersey line; it could be heard for a mile square.

Without Mac I would have lived a much quieter life. Sometimes I wished for that. Other times, like for my fifteenth birthday, when he pulled the fire alarm and had the school evacuated so I didn't have to take a chemistry exam, I loved him more than anyone.

It was a bad summer. I had second-degree burns, mostly on my back, and they didn't hurt too much, but sometimes they stung when I tried to move too quickly. Mac didn't apologize for anything that summer, for the burns or the disappearances or the time we spent apart, and I didn't expect him to. He left a pack of cigarettes on my windowsill instead, one Sunday in the very early morning when I was still asleep, but it rained and they were soaked through. I kept the packet and pressed it under a book like a dried flower until it was thin as an eggshell, and then I built a frame for it using my father's woodworking equipment. I hung it above my bed in my room.

By the middle of summer, it was clear Mac's mother wasn't getting any better. It wasn't so much that she was sick as that she was crazy, crazier like what you see on TV or read about in magazines with a flashlight after your parents have gone to bed. She had always been a little bit crazy, and my dad said it ran in their family, which meant that Mac might be crazy too. My dad had gone to high school with some of Mac's uncles, and he said they were all a bit off. "I wish you wouldn't spend so much time with that boy," my dad said, and I agreed.

In the kitchen that morning, my dad and I circled each other like cats, scrapping over the bacon and eggs, while my mother tried to keep the peace. He and I hadn't spoken the same language in several years and struggled to understand one another. My mother plied my father with more coffee and me with second helpings of everything. I had started growing that summer, and I was voracious.

"Mac hasn't done anything bad to Lillian," my mother said. "It's good that she has a friend in the neighborhood." She was kind enough to ignore that I didn't have friends at school either. My mother was the tactful one in our family.

She put the coffee pot in front of my father. My father had problems with Mac, ever since I was a kid. When I was eleven, I broke my hand punching Mac in the face. He told me, "Hit me in the face as hard as you can." He had just read *Fight Club.* My parents took me to the hospital, incredulous.

"Why would you do something like that?" my mother had asked me.

"He told me to do it," I said, cradling my broken hand in my lap.

"Would you do anything he told you to? If he walked off a cliff, would you walk off after him?" my father asked.

"No," I said because I had the good sense to lie. But the truth was, if Mac had wanted to walk off a cliff, I would have waddled after him.

My father grabbed the bacon. "Are you kidding?" he said. "He's been after her since they were kids. The burns. And the gallivanting around at night. And you know he's the reason why she's missed so much school, Sarah. I know that's not just a funny coincidence."

I reached around and touched my back where the burns were healing, shiny and pink. My father had tried grounding me to keep me away from Mac, but he showed up at our house every Saturday, expecting me, regardless of whether I was allowed to go out. "She hasn't missed that much school," my mother said. She passed the bacon back to me. "Sam, you're overreacting. Just be glad she has friends."

My father colored the bruised shade of an old apple. "The neighbors don't say anything good about him." My father was a notorious gossip and mostly worked from home. He spent an awful lot of time sitting on the porch with the neighborhood ladies, drinking iced tea and eating cookies, while my mother was at work. He was a woodworker, and he taught me the trade from a young age. It was one of the only ways we related to one another. I wasn't particularly interested in carpentry, but it was better than doing nothing on a Sunday afternoon.

"Never mind the neighbors," my mother said. "Lillian is fine, Sam. She's just growing up."

"I just don't like the look of that boy," my father said. He never called Mac by his real name. "I wish she'd spend more time with girls her own age."

"We all want things, Sam," my mother said.

I stared into my bacon and eggs.

*

"Jesus was a carpenter," Mac pointed out later that morning, after his father had left for work and he had nothing to do. Mac had left a bottle of cheap wine on the garage floor when he had come in, but he hadn't opened it.

"Are you saying that my dad is Jesus?" I asked. Mac had a strange affinity for my father, even though my father despised him.

"He's definitely closer to God than my dad," Mac said. His dark hair fell in his eyes. He was inspecting one of his cigarettes for a defect.

"If my dad is Jesus, does that make me an angel or what?"

Mac tossed a piece of scrap wood at me and missed. I winced. His aim could be lethal when he was in the right mood, but he was mellow this morning. "You're no angel," he said but didn't explain himself further. "My mom's not coming home this week."

His mother was in the hospital. Psych ward, my father said. I had watched when they had taken her away, kicking and screaming, in the back of an ambulance. Mac had gotten in after her. I had watched them drive away, the ambulance getting smaller and smaller and then disappearing.

"I heard my dad tell my mom that Mrs. Hall said she was getting worse. The doctors said she's not even lucid."

It was dangerous to provoke Mac with talk of his mother, but he was the one who brought it up. He would have been even more livid if I had told him a lie or changed the subject. Mac liked to test people, and the best method against this was always honesty. "She's lucid," Mac said. "She knew my name.

She knew I was her son. It's the hospital—it's making her confused. They're giving her too many drugs."

From what I knew about Mac's mom, she had always been a few sticks short of a bundle. Half the time, when we were little, she barely recognized me, and the other half the time she called me Jill. She was always nice enough, but forgetful; Mac had to remind her to turn the stove off or take the laundry out of the dryer. Sometimes she spent the whole day, fully dressed, lying in the queen bed in Mac's parents' room until his father came home from work.

"Well if she's still sick, you can't take her out of the hospital," I pointed out. I was fiddling with the leg of a chair I had built. Mac lit his cigarette and exhaled a cloud of blue smoke. He began systematically lighting wood shavings on fire with his green plastic lighter and watching them burn.

"You should really get a new hobby," he said. "Guys don't like girls who are only interested in playing with pieces of wood."

"You're changing the subject," I said.

"Actually, you're right," he said. "Some guys might be into that."

I ignored his dirty joke. "Your mom," I said. "Do you want me to come and visit her with you?"

"We won't need to visit her," he said, shaking his head. "She's coming home."

I didn't argue. It was impossible to change his mind when he got like this.

*

I walked into the living room where my father was watching the news. Mac had wandered off, saying something about needing to go home before his father got home from work, and I was alone.

"How's that boy?" my father said, not taking his eyes off the television.

"He's fine." I sat down next to him on the couch. When I was a kid, my father and I had gone on outings on the weekends: Chuck E. Cheese, the county fair. Now we barely spoke.

"You didn't touch any of my tools in the garage, did you?"

My father was perpetually terrified that we would do something to one of his power saws, like permanently maim ourselves. "No," I said. "We didn't touch any of your tools."

My mother came in from the kitchen. "Dinner is almost ready," she said, looking at the two of us on the couch. "It's so nice to see the two of you getting along."

"We're just sitting," my father said, looking defensive. "Can't a man sit in his own house without it being commented on?"

"Jesus," my mother said. "I was just saying it's nice to see the two of you together. That's all."

"Yeah," I said. "It is nice."

My father looked at me, stunned. I remembered, suddenly, what it was like to hold his hand as we walked into Chuck E. Cheese, what it felt like to push those little metal tokens into the slots to play games, how we split a funnel cake at the county fair and he won me a stuffed toy frog. I shook off the feeling. I wasn't a little girl anymore.

"Okay," my father said finally. "I guess I'm the minority here. And possibly the only person in this family who hasn't gone completely insane."

I thought of Mac's mother, who was actually insane and being held in a locked ward. "I don't think it's nice to talk about crazy people that way," I said and got up to wash my hands for dinner.

Mac knocked on my window that night around three in the morning. I was awake, sanding down the legs of a table I had built the weekend before. I had stained it black and filled my room with noxious fumes. When I couldn't sleep, I messed around with furniture.

Mac had a lit cigarette in his mouth and dropped ash all over my windowsill as he clambered up the drainpipe. His face was familiar, even in the dark. "What are you doing?"

"Can't sleep." I handed him an ashtray that I had made out of a spare piece of basswood. Mac rarely came inside my house, but when he was here, I was prepared for him. He flicked on the light switch and flooded the room with light. I had been working with my desk lamp and blinked hard, adjusting to the transition. "What are you doing?"

"I was in the neighborhood, thought I'd stop by." He knocked ash off of the end of his cigarette into the ashtray on the windowsill. "Nice picture frame."

I looked over at where I had hung the frame with his cigarette packet. "Thanks."

"Didn't think you would have kept that," he said.

"Well, you know."

"Know what?"

I didn't say anything.

"Anyways," he said finally. "Do you want to go on a walk with me?"

I thought about the last time we had gone on a walk. It had ended up with my hair singed and his nose broken. It had healed slightly crooked, although only I could tell.

It wasn't unusual for Mac to show up at weird hours unannounced. Sometimes he brought a bottle of something, and we sat in the treehouse, watching the trees from a little slit between the boards. Sometimes we walked to the reservoir, and if it was warm enough, Mac would swim. Once we went to a party, which was disastrous. Weeks would go by where he wouldn't drop in, and sometimes he was here every night. Usually he threw something at the window or whistled loudly. It was strange for him to come all the way inside.

"Come on," he said. "I've got a good idea. I don't want to go by myself. It'll be fun."

He crushed his cigarette in the ashtray. I stood up and put on my sneakers.

It was raining, but quietly, the way it rains in summer. Mac's hair was plastered to his forehead, his damp T-shirt sticking to his back. My shoes squelched across the grass as we cut through Mrs. Welsh's lawn, down Crabapple Street, and toward town. Our suburb spread widely around a little knot of shops, all within walking distance. We passed the shops fast, dark, silent storefronts looming and then disappearing. I couldn't tell where we're going, not yet.

"You want to know where we're going, right?" Mac asked. We were off the pedestrian path and walking along the road now, out of the town center. There was the mall, but I couldn't imagine why he would want to go there; it was the middle of the night.

"I don't care," I said.

"You sure?" In a snakelike motion, Mac grabbed ahold of my ponytail and twisted it. Immediately I struck out with the palm of my hand, catching him under the jaw. He yelped and let go.

There was a silence, and then he laughed, a horrible, harsh sound. I didn't want to be with him all of a sudden. "Gosh, Lil," he said, pivoting on his heel. "I was just testing your reflexes. Besides, it's too wet out for fire, remember?"

I surged forward suddenly, went in for a kiss, and missed, catching the side of his rough cheek. It made a wet sucking sound that embarrassed both of us. I pulled back, shy, tentative, and kept walking forward.

"So that's the way it's going to be," Mac said.

The day that Mac had lit my hair on fire earlier that summer, it had been hot, so humid you could cut the air with a butter knife. It was too hot to stay in the garage, too hot to go outside, too hot to do anything except lie on the ground, waiting for the heat to dissipate. When Mac had said, "Let's go to the reservoir," I agreed, simply for something to distract from the heat.

Mac had been sipping wine all day, which I couldn't imagine doing; it must have made him so hot. He was in a dangerous mood, black and cloudy, and I was wary around him. When he got like this, there was no stopping him. He would destroy everything in his wake.

The reservoir was low that year because of the heat, too low to swim in. There was a neighborhood pool, but it was crowded and loud and cramped, the water chemical-smelling and foul. Someone vomited in the pool at least once a week, and they were constantly picking dead frogs out of the drains.

I knew Mac's mother had gone into the hospital, but I didn't know how to ask him about it. Everyone in the neighborhood knew. She hadn't exactly gone quietly. "How are you?" I asked as we walked onto the stretch of cement that surrounded the reservoir. It was disguised as a lake, but there was a little strip of concrete at the end where we usually stretched out, dipping our feet in the water.

"Never better," he said, pulling a bottle of red wine out of his backpack. I recognized it as the one my father had been saving since Christmas but didn't say anything. "Come on. It's a beautiful day. What is there to complain about?"

"I don't know," I said. "It's so hot. And I mean, your mom."

He took a slug from the bottle of wine and shrugged. "So what?"

"I meant," I said. "Are you okay? About her?"

"Of course I'm okay," he said shortly. His lighter was in his hand, and he was flicking it, over and over. "Why wouldn't I be okay?"

"Mac?"

"Yes?" He turned toward me, and for an instant I thought he was going to kiss me, he looked at me so tenderly. Then he grabbed my braid, and the smell of singed hair was in the air. It didn't burn quickly or easily, but it stung my back where my shoulders were exposed and sent sparks flying down, striking the back of my legs. I pulled at my ponytail with my bare hands and finally plunged my head into the reservoir, extinguishing the fire. Mac watched silently.

I sat on the bank of the reservoir and cut the singed part out of my hair with my pocketknife. Mac was quiet, drinking, but his eyes followed me. I had burnt red patches on my back and legs.

"Why did you do that?" I asked quietly. I felt strangely calm. It wouldn't hurt, not until much later. I stood up, made like I was going to head home. I was going to head home. I don't know if I expected an answer. Mac rarely directed his fury at me. Other people, sure, but never me.

He had gathered his things up by that point. The wine bottle was in his backpack. As I watched, he buckled over and threw up. It was red and looked like blood. When he was finished, he straightened, wiped his mouth with the back of his hand, and fixed me with a strange stare. "You were there," he said.

When I punched him, I heard the crack of bone under my hand. I saw the blood gush from his nose and felt his face turn up into a smile.

My parents asked about the burns, of course. I told my father I had spilled some wood stain on my back, and then Mac had accidentally lit it on fire with one of his cigarettes. I could tell my dad didn't believe me, but it was easier to nod and say, "all right," than press me for answers. My dad didn't like confrontation. My mother rubbed aloe on my burns, and my father sat in the kitchen, simmering.

"I just wish you wouldn't spend so much time with that boy," he said when I came out of the bathroom that night. "He's dangerous."

"He's harmless," I said, thinking of the time I had seen Mac threaten a younger boy with a knife. "He would never really hurt me."

"I just don't think that's true, Lillian. And I don't want you to see him anymore. Do you understand me?"

"I understand," I said, although my father could just have easily asked two magnets not to attract one another. I knew I would still see Mac. No one could keep us apart. We would just have to be sneakier about it.

"Mac," I said, rubbing water out of my eyes. "Where are we going?"

We had been walking for an hour. I couldn't recognize any landmarks because of the rain, which was falling more steadily now. Mac's T-shirt was sticking to his long, lean body. I tried not to look at the plane of his stomach, which heaved when he breathed.

"We're going to go get my mother," he said.

"At the hospital? Mac, that's miles," I said. "And besides, isn't she still sick?"

"She's not sick, she's fine," Mac said.

"If she's in the hospital, I don't think she's fine," I said.

Mac stopped walking. "If I say she's fine, she's fine," he said. "Since when do you question me?"

He was right. I rarely did. "I'm sorry," I said.

He looked at me. I could tell something was coming, but I didn't know what. Mac exhaled in one long, slow breath, like he was smoking a cigarette. "She tried to kill herself," he said. "That's why she's in the hospital. Okay? Are you happy now? She tried to leave me, leave all of us." His voice broke. "Is that what you wanted to hear?"

"Mac," I said. "I'm so sorry. I didn't know."

"I know you didn't know," he snapped. "And now they're holding her against her will. So we're going to go get her. She doesn't want to be in that place, Lil."

I didn't think the hospital people were just going to let us walk out with his mother, but I didn't say that. "I'm sorry," I said again.

"It's fine," he said, although it wasn't. "Just—just promise you won't leave me, Lil. Promise me you won't try and leave me like she did. You're my only friend." His voice broke again. "Don't leave me alone with my father."

"I won't," I said. "I promise."

When we got to the hospital, hours later, it was still raining. We were both soaking wet. Mac looked at me, eyes bright.

The sun was just starting to rise. I thought about walking home, but it seemed wrong to leave him here in the parking lot. We had been through so much together. I watched as he smoked a cigarette, slow, under the awning for the emergency room.

We went inside. At the front desk, Mac told the guard that he was here to visit his mother.

"Visiting hours don't start for another few hours," the guard said. "You'll have to come back in the morning."

"It is the morning," Mac said. "The sun is up." I recognized the glint in his eye. He moved his hand toward his pocket, chest heaving.

"Mac, don't," I said, but he already had his Bic lighter in his hand.

Wish You Were Here

Jon tells me not to want anymore. I want him, more than I want anything. I want not to want him. I want to want nothing.

He is a live wire. I am the nail, a second before the hammer hits it.

We are not a couple. He is thirty-four. I am twenty, not old enough to drink, but old enough to enlist in the military, which I can't. I have flat feet, and I couldn't pass the psych eval. We met in the psych ward. Jon was there because he tried to kill himself. I was there because I tried to kill my ex-boyfriend, Wilbur.

"Come here," Jon says.

"Okay," I say.

I like Jon because I cannot hurt him. He is beyond hurt. He has renounced everything: food, sex, love. We lie in his bed and stare at the ceiling. Sometimes we do drugs. We measure time in cigarettes.

I am surprised by how clear everything is. "You're drunk," Jon says when I tell him this.

"Yes," I say.

Jon will not fuck me. He says it would ruin everything. I want him to want me, but more than that, I want him to kiss me the way he did in the summer, like I would break. Jon and I used to do it, but we stopped. I don't know why. We stopped, and now it's impossible to start again.

"We should just do it," I tell him. "Come on. It won't be that hard."

Jon kisses me. His mouth is cold. "No," he says. "I don't think so."

Jon is taking a vow of celibacy. Jon is becoming a monk. Jon is transcending.

"I hate you," I say. I roll over on my side. I try to sleep. I will not sleep.

Jon holds me. "It's okay," he says.

"No, it's not," I say.

Jon and I go out for drinks. I am already drunk. Jon says I am always drunk when I see him. This is true; he has figured out my secret. "Fine," I say when I sit down. I order us two tequila shots. The bartender gives me a dirty look. He hates me. I don't care.

"Okay," Jon says and does the shot. He makes a face.

"Pussy," I say. I do mine without making a face.

"You're drunk," he says.

"You always say that," I say.

"You always are." He lights a cigarette. "And you always yell at me."

"I do not," I say. "I'm just sexually frustrated."

"You're fucking at least three other people."

"But I'm in love with you," I say.

"I don't believe you," he says. "You're always drunk when you say that."

"What, do you want me to make myself throw up and then say it?" I say.

"I don't think drinking works like that," he says. "Look, I'm not going to stay here if you're just going to fight with me."

"Okay, okay," I say. "I'm not going to fight." I get up off my stool and go over and kiss him on the cheek. He turns his face and kisses me on the lips, which I wasn't asking for.

"Why'd you do that?"

"What?"

"Nothing."

We talk about nothing for a while. Then we start fighting again. Later we go back to his place, lie around, watch YouTube videos. I fall asleep on the couch. Around one in the morning, Jon kicks me out.

"You don't even know me," Jon says when I pick him up from his house on Saturday morning. I am sober, tired, hungover.

"I know you," I say. He's grinning like something good happened. I hate him. He glows.

He cracks his jaw. "Uh."

I light a cigarette. We walk toward the breakfast place. We're supposed to be having a nonalcoholic interaction. I don't know what to say to him.

In the hospital, it was easy to talk to him. I was on a lot of pills. Words floated by like balloons. I grabbed onto their strings and tugged on them. Jon told me secrets and stories and made me laugh.

I miss that time. I want to go back there. Jon will never go back there. I know that about him.

"Why did you try to kill yourself?" I say. He doesn't seem like the type. He's too cool.

"I don't know," he says after thinking about it for a while. "It seemed like the thing to do at the time."

I pick at my eggs. Jon is smiling, tapping his fingers on the table. "Why are you so happy?" I ask.

"I like being around you," he says.

"Then why won't you just do it with me?" I say.

He sighs, rolls his eyes. "I've told you this one already," he says. "It would make everything so much more complicated. Besides, I don't think we do it right."

"Right?"

"Right."

I want a cigarette. Instead I lean over and kiss Jon, who hesitates, then kisses me back. His mouth is dry. He doesn't seem like he wants to. I pull back, look at his face. His pupils are huge—he's high. He's always high.

"Okay," he says.

"Okay, what?"

"Just, okay."

We go back to his place after that. I strip off his T-shirt, then his pants. He gets me out of my shorts in record time. I'm not wearing underwear—laundry day. My lipstick gets all over my face. His tongue tastes like cigarettes. I suck on it.

He's right about one thing though.

We really don't do it right.

After, lying in his bed on his clean sheets, comforter wrapped around my legs, I shake my head. "Things really aren't any more complicated than they already were," I say.

"I guess not," he says. He looks uncomfortable, but also tired. And happy.

"So I was right."

"I don't know," he says. He reaches over me to get his cigarettes and lights one, then passes them to me.

"I would never do anything to hurt you," I say.

"I know that," he says. "I know."

"But you would hurt me," I say.

"Only if you wanted me to." His grin is wicked.

"Oh, shut up."

He sits up, grabs my wrists, cigarette hanging out of his mouth at an angle. "I wouldn't," he says.

"Okay," I say.

Somehow, some way, I fall asleep.

*

Sometimes we take a break. Sometimes it gets to be too much, and I don't see Jon for a little while.

I write Jon a postcard. I drop it in his mailbox. "Wish you were here," it says.

A week later, he writes me back.

"I am here," he says.

"Okay," I write back.

"Okay," he writes back.

Sleeping With the Kinds of Boys Who Wouldn't Talk to Me in High School

Hallways and highways. Endless hills. Dr Pepper Lipsmackers. Grady's hands on my thighs. People ask me sometimes, what were you like back then? I don't know what to tell them. I was like this, I tell them, but it's a lie. I wasn't like anything. I was too tall for my age and thirteen and gangly and awkward, and he was the only one who saw me. If my brother, away at college, had known, he would have killed us both.

I am thirty. I turn thirty this year. It's a strange age—another fifteen years, and I will be middle-aged, but fifteen years ago, I was a child. And I am successful, I think. Everyone says so. My picture has been on the cover of magazines. I've walked in Fashion Week after Fashion Week. People ask in interviews: How did you know you were special? Did you know at a young age?

No, I tell them. I didn't think I was anything.

Only Grady saw me, I want to say. But then I'd have to explain about me and him, and being thirteen when he was twenty, and all the nights in his pickup truck, together under a wool blanket, and my mouth dries up.

He and my brother were friends. He was a year older than my brother, had dropped out. There were rumors about him. That he sold drugs. Don't let that Stern boy around our house, my father said. My father said a lot of things. Mostly he said things like, get me another bourbon, Kitty (to my mother), or he said, get out of my way, or he said, shit.

Sometimes my father acted like he cared about me. I was an accident. He didn't want my brother, and he didn't want me. He felt like my mother had trapped him by having kids. He took me hunting when I was a kid, but he stopped when I broke my arm when I fell out of a tree. Well, my mother made him stop. It'll make her tough, he said when they had the fight about it in the kitchen that night.

She's tough enough, my mother said.

Most of the time my parents ignored me. They ignored my brother too. When my brother got big enough, they told him: Big one, watch the little one, and then they left us to our own devices. My brother was five years older than me. My mother didn't like kids and had my brother only because she thought it was the only way to keep my father around. When she got pregnant with me, she figured, well, why not? She wasn't well suited to motherhood. She was more likely to burn water than boil it, and her idea of a fun family night was to plop us in front of the TV and then go out on the porch to smoke cigarettes.

My brother and I had a lot of fun on our own. We played boys versus girls, cowboys and Indians, hide-and-seek, all on the half-acre or so of farmland that our little house was built on. The land was the only thing that my father had to give us, left over from his father's much larger farm in the 1950s. Most of the land had been sold, but we still had this little strip to play on. We ducked through rotting cornfields, hid in the woods, waded through the creek that ran halfway through our property and onto the next one, and got so covered in mud that our mother threw up her hands in exasperation and went outside to get the hose.

But my brother got older. By the time I was ten or eleven, he was in high school and wasn't interested in playing with me anymore. He had Grady and his new friends who drove fast down the curving roads that ran through our town while smoking cigarettes and who knew what else. Then it was just me, wandering aimlessly through the fields with a stick in hand, turning over rocks to see if I could find newts or lizards. I never could.

I don't know how my brother met Grady. I never asked, and he never told me. We didn't really talk. We drove, and I would smoke his menthols, stretching my too long legs out on the dashboard. Before Grady picked me up, he would pick my brother up. Then my brother went to college. He appeared in our driveway one Sunday and said, Hey, Tessa.

Yeah? I said.

You wanna go for a drive? he said.

I looked behind me. My mother was in the kitchen, washing dishes. My father was in the living room, watching football. My brother was away at college. I had done all my homework.

OK, I said.

We drove for a while, and eventually he pulled over in a field.

You know about sex, right? he said, handing me a cigarette.

I knew about smoking because I had stolen some cigarettes from my mother and tried them when I was eleven. I lit the cigarette with the lighter he gave me and took a long drag and nodded. Uh-huh, I said.

We were sitting in the cab of his truck. I still remember that truck. It was red and always smelled like smoke. Good, Grady said.

He was pretty, even then. Long eyelashes. Do you want me to show you how to do it? he asked me.

I guess so, I said. If you want to.

You have to want me to, he said. Or else it won't work right.

I thought about it. Smoked my cigarette. Thought about the girls in my grade, eighth, who had sex. They were the ones who were developed already, the ones who wore more than training bras and had boyfriends and smoked cigarettes behind the school and talked to high school boys.

Grady was better than a high school boy. He could have been a college boy, he was old enough. So what if people said he sold drugs? I had heard from someone that he cut someone's thumbs off once. I looked at him, at his body.

Do you want me to touch you? he said.

I can't explain what it was about that time. It was like I didn't have thoughts. Like I didn't know how to think yet. When I moved to New York, I started sleeping with the kinds of boys who wouldn't talk to me in high school. Finance majors; blond, blue-eyed boys; nonsmokers. They always told me I was beautiful, and I guess I was. Grady never said that.

When you're that age, you pretty much do what adults say. I remember moving to New York, and someone asked me if I wanted French or ranch on my salad, and I couldn't decide. No one had ever asked me what I wanted before. They had just assumed.

Yeah, I said. I want you to touch me.

OK, he said.

At school no one would talk to me. I was nearly six feet tall at thirteen and wore size eleven shoes and didn't need to wear a bra. I was a freak. People whispered about me in the halls. My brother had been a football player, a good one, and people knew I was his sister.

Why are you so weird? Amanda asked me after gym one day. Your brother was cool.

I don't know, I said.

She looked at me like I was dog shit she had just stepped in. Oh, she said.

My ex-fiancé wanted to know details. I didn't want to give him details. You don't want to know, I said. It was just a thing that happened.

We lay in bed together, not touching. You have to tell me, he said.

I don't have to tell you anything, I said. It's personal. It happened to me, just me.

We're getting married, he said. You're supposed to tell me everything.

He wanted justice. He wanted to find Grady, to prosecute him. I tried to tell him about statutes of limitations, about proof. About evidence. There is no physical proof that anything happened. All there is are my memories. I can never forget what happened. I don't want to forget what happened.

Except sometimes. Sometimes I want to forget so much.

I think people always assume that because I am beautiful, I'll be happy. I'm not unhappy, but I wouldn't say I'm happy either. I think it's easier for ugly people actually. When you're pretty, everyone expects more of you. They think, oh, there goes that pretty girl. They think you'll do something important.

The truth was, I didn't want to get a real job. I had no skills. I didn't have the grades to get into college. When the recruiter in the mall offered me the contract, I didn't have to think about it. I said okay, and two weeks later, I was getting off the bus on 34th Street.

I know I'm lucky. Not everyone is successful at this. I've been very fortunate. Now that I'm retired, I don't do much. I paint a little, watercolors. I talk to my mother, my brother, on the phone. I talk to people. I think.

*

Why does there have to be a why? I ask myself sometimes. Why are we like this?

I didn't know what was happening. Not really. I wasn't a person yet, and though I thought I was very grown up, smoking my cigarettes with my legs up, shoes off, driving through the backroads of rural Indiana, I wasn't anything other than a thirteen-year-old girl playing older. He knew better. I didn't. At some point someone needs to be held accountable.

But who?

Some nights we would drive into Indianapolis, go to dinner. He would pay. I never asked where he got the money—he didn't work, not in the traditional sense. I think he did sell drugs. Sometimes we would meet his friends in the city, and they would go off somewhere for a few minutes, and I would wait in the car, and he would come back glassy-eyed and hyper, and he would want to kiss me, and I would let him. He would kiss the space between my neck and collarbone, and I would fall back into the seat, and the world would open up.

I don't know why I never asked any questions. I didn't ask how he knew my brother. I didn't ask what he was doing with his friends. I didn't ask for any drugs, although sometimes he would give me pills, and we would share them in the front seat of the car. Once we did a hit of acid and spent the whole night watching the sky breathe. My mother almost never asked me where I was. I think she was just glad I was out of the house and out of her hair.

Why are you always so tired in class? my history teacher, Mr. Beeman, asked me.

My dad, he watches TV with the volume loud, I said.

Can't you ask him to turn it down?

You can't ask my dad to do anything, I said.

Some nights I did try to sleep, I really did. I stared at the ceiling and wished for Grady to come and rescue me. I had elaborate fantasies where we got into the truck and drove and drove until we reached the ocean. And then the car would turn into a boat, and we would speed away and never look back. I didn't care about my parents. I guessed that I would miss my brother, but he could visit us wherever we ended up.

My brother called a few times a month and told us how he was doing. He was at IU, studying engineering. He had a football scholarship. I was really proud of him.

Come rescue me, I told him.

OK, he said.

But he never did.

People ask me now, were you a cheerleader? Did you do gymnastics? People assume that models are born beautiful. The truth is, you are what you make of yourself. I spent hours in my apartment, my shithole apartment in Brooklyn that I shared with four other models, looking at my face in the mirror. Finding my angles. Thinking of Grady's voice in my ear, his breath on my neck.

Of course, I was eighteen, and I hadn't seen him in years. He had moved away from town by then. He left the summer I turned sixteen, but we hadn't spoken in years. I noticed his leaving the way you notice that the sun sets—all at once, it had just happened. I wasn't sad about it, not in the traditional sense. There was nothing to be sad about. To be sad about something, you have to have lost something. I hadn't lost anything because there was nothing there at all.

I remember when I first learned that you could make a man do what you wanted just by turning your head a certain way, wearing a certain lipstick, pursing your lips. I practiced in the mirror in my childhood bedroom with lipstick stolen from my mother. By the time I was seventeen, I had started to look older, objectively good-looking, my teenage awkwardness molding into something almost pretty. I never had much in the way of breasts, but some people want that. Some people want the childish frame, the long legs, the frizzy hair. There's someone out there for everyone.

I used to drive into Indianapolis on my own, wearing cocktail dresses I had purchased at thrift stores on the edge of town, red lipstick, and I would sit in bars and watch men twice my age fall over themselves to talk to me. It was easy. It reminded me of Grady actually. I would tilt my head to the side, and the businessman from Arkansas would come over and buy me martinis and ask me if I wanted to go to his hotel room, and I would laugh and say, sorry, no. No, thank you. Thanks for the drink.

And then I would walk out of the bars, head held high, smiling.

It was days like this that I wanted to call Grady. I never did of course. But I wanted to call him, send him pictures of what I looked like now, and tell him: Look at me. Look at what I've become. When I moved to New York, I thought about that a lot. I wanted to say, you saw me then. Now look at me. See what everyone else sees now.

I asked him once, why don't you hang out with girls your own age?

You're mature for your age, he said. We were sitting in the back of the truck, passing a cigarette back and forth. My pants were around my ankles. He was breathing heavy. I don't know. I like hanging out with you.

We don't do anything, I said. We just drive and fuck and smoke.

Is there anything else to do? he said. What, do you want to go to the fucking movies?

I looked at his profile. It was dark, the kind of dark you only get in the country, that complete total darkness. When I moved to the city, I missed it. But I could see his nose, the shape of his chin.

I don't know, I said. I just wondered.

Well, don't, he said.

Sometimes he was rough. I didn't mind. I never have. I want them to hurt me, I think. I don't know why. It reminds me that I'm here, I guess. That I'm real. That I'm more than just a collection of symptoms. That I exist.

I'm here, I panted as he twisted my arm. I'm here. I'm here.

I know, he said. I know.

Rocking back and forth in the cab of the truck. Right at the last second, he would pull away from me, finish on the hot metal.

Don't want any little guys running around, he would say. Laugh. Light a cigarette.

He would take three drags, pass it to me. I would touch my new bruises and smoke and think about the girls in my gym class, the ones who called me a freak. I wondered what they did with their boyfriends, if they did this. I kind of thought they didn't. They were too scared, they wouldn't let anyone touch them, not for years. I felt brave. Strong. Tough.

My father always said, I didn't raise no little bitch. Then he would spit, even if we were inside.

No, you didn't, I thought to myself. No, you didn't, Daddy.

What are you thinking about? Grady asked me. He didn't usually ask me direct questions, except do you like that, baby?

Nothing, I said.

Okay.

He buttoned his shirt. I looked at the skin of his throat. He was beautiful, straight nose, clear skin. Blue eyes like something else. I didn't know what he was doing with me, didn't want to know. But I knew.

Because I was there.

*

Afterward we would go get McDonald's. Burgers, fries, Cokes. Eat in the car, pulled over by the side of the road. The salt burned my lips.

Do you like that, baby?

Uh-huh.

The night outside the car, still and quiet. Then he would drive me home, and my mother would ask me where I had been, and I would tell her, out, and go upstairs and take a shower, a hot one, and go to bed.

I've never told anyone about this. No one has ever asked. These days, when I want sex, I go to a bar, sit down, and wait. Someone always comes up to me. Sex is easy. Bodies are easy. They're like envelopes. Carrying cases, made for being easily discarded. I lose mine easily. I don't care about sex. It never feels like anything to me, not really, not anymore.

Sometimes someone asks me to tell them: Tell me about the first time you fell in love.

Well, I say.

The girls in the hallway were always mean. Some times were worse than others. They couldn't physically hurt me, the way they pushed some girls around, because I was bigger than they were, but they could be cruel.

Why are you so fucking tall? they asked. Why don't you wear a bra? What, are you a boy? Do you have a dick?

Let's see it.

And then they'd attack me in the locker room. Showering for gym became an ordeal. Towels snapped, tampons thrown, my clothes hidden.

No boys ever asked me to dances. I didn't have friends. No one wanted to talk to me at lunch. Mostly I ate in the library in between the stacks.

But I didn't care. I had my secret, my nights in Grady's pickup. That was all I needed. We could lie back and look at the stars and smoke weed, and I could feel infinite, even if it was just for a few moments.

Thanksgiving. I turned fourteen on Thanksgiving. My brother came home from college with a beard and a new girlfriend. Her name was Sophia, and I didn't like her. She was a cheerleader. Dumb as a box of rocks, as they say.

You're tall, she said when she met me.

You're short, I said.

Tessa, my mother said. Don't be rude.

It was my birthday, but I had to have family dinner with everyone. I wanted to be alone. My brother punched me on the shoulder and said, what's up, kid.

I've been fucking your friend, I didn't say. In the bed of his pickup truck. We don't talk either. We just do it, and then he takes me home.

My brother and his girlfriend went outside to smoke a joint. I wanted some but didn't know how to ask without making it into a thing. My father got drunk. My mother fussed in the kitchen.

In the midst of all this, Grady's truck pulled up in the driveway. My brother came out from behind the house and gave him a hug. They clapped each other on the back.

I'm here for Tessa's birthday, Grady said.

I went outside onto the porch. Hi, I said.

Grady gave me a cigarette.

You're smoking now? my brother said.

Uh-huh.

Grady, she's thirteen.

Fourteen, I said.

I lit the cigarette, took a drag. My brother looked at me. Looked at Grady. What's going on here? he asked.

Nothing, Grady said. Nothing at all. Tessa, do you want to take a drive with me?

We're having dinner, my brother said.

Matthew, who is this? Sophia said.

Grady stuck out his hand. Grady Stern, at your service.

I don't know what you're talking about, she said.

We're having dinner, I said to Grady. Sorry.

Raincheck, he said. He smiled that big smile, the one where you could see his gold tooth. I dropped the cigarette butt on the ground, crushed it with my heel. Grady gave my brother a nod. I see college has been treating you well, brother.

I'm not your brother, he said.

Right, Grady said. Well, you know what I meant.

I don't know about that.

Sophia crinkled her little nose. What's going on, Matthew? she said.

Nothing, my brother said. Go back in the house.

I thought you'd be happy to see me, Grady said.

I thought so too, my brother said. Look. Just stay away from my sister, okay? That's all.

Grady looked at me. Tell your sister to stay away from me, he said.

My brother made his hands into fists. Man, he said. I really don't want to beat your ass right now. It's Thanksgiving. She's goddamn fourteen.

Grady held his hands out. Whatever, man, he said. Whatever you say.

He got back in his truck and drove away. My brother looked at me. That guy gives you any trouble, you talk to me, okay? I'm just an hour away.

Uh-huh, I said.

We went back into the house.

There was only one time I was ever scared.

Grady drove up one night and looked at me in my cutoffs and T-shirt and said, get dressed. Something better than that.

Like what?

Hang on. He parked the truck and said, can I come in?

Uh-huh.

My mother was asleep. I let him in through the back door, and we went up to my room. He seemed too large for my room. He went to my closet, pawed through my clothes, and pulled out a dress I had only worn to funerals.

Here.

I put it on, swiped my lips with lip gloss.

Good.

We got into the truck. I didn't ask where we were going. I smoked a cigarette. Grady drove one-handed, taking backroads. We approached the city, lights coming up ahead of us. I need you to keep your mouth shut, Grady said as we pulled into a parking spot in front of an apartment building. Just do what I say, and you'll be fine.

OK, I said.

Good.

We went upstairs. There were three men in the apartment. It was dark in there, smelled bad. There were a lot of drugs on the coffee table, I don't know what. Maybe crystal meth. Grady picked up a baggie of something and took some money out of his pocket and gave it to one of the men.

Who's your friend? one of the men said.

This is Tessa.

Hiya, sweetheart.

Hi, I said.

Tessa, honey, do you want a drink?

No, thank you, I said.

Tessa, baby, how old are you? someone said.

Don't say anything, Grady said. She's old enough.

Raised eyebrows.

The men eyeing me. The bad smell. I tugged on Grady's sleeve. Can I have a cigarette?

He gave me one. I smoked it, dropping ash into an empty beer can. I sat on the couch, which was velvet and smelled like mold. A man sitting next to me tried to put his hand on my thigh. Grady looked at him, and he stopped. But he kept asking me questions.

I'm still in school, I told him.

College?

No, I said. And then I lied: high school.

You look older.

I get that a lot, I said, even though I didn't. Everyone always said I looked young. I was just tall.

You seem older too. You've got a good way about you.

Grady was doing lines of whatever it was off a mirror on the table. I didn't know how long we were staying here. I didn't know why he had brought me here at all. This wasn't what we did. What we did was drive around, fuck, smoke cigarettes. Sometimes we drank a little whiskey from a silver flask he kept in the glove box of his truck. Sometimes we got dinner.

Are you his girl? the man asked me.

I don't know, I said. I guess so. I looked at Grady. Am I?

Damn right, you're my girl. Possessive look. Gritted teeth. Stay away from her, Elmo.

All right, all right.

She costs more than you'll ever have anyway.

Where did you even find her?

They were talking about me like I wasn't even there.

Grady? I said. I have to, um, use the bathroom.

Down the hall, sweetheart.

I got up, walked down the dark hallway. A cat ran down the hall in front of me, startling me. I turned on the bathroom light, a single bulb. It swayed, casting a greenish light over everything. I looked at myself in the mirror. Wide eyes, pale, scared-looking face. Frizzy hair in a halo. Too skinny. Shoulder blades. I squatted down on the dirty toilet, peed, washed my hands. Splashed some cold water on my face, redid my lip gloss. Then I went back outside.

Can we go?

We're just getting started, one of the men said.

Grady stood up. Uh-huh, he said. Are you sure?

Yeah, I'm sure, I said.

Oh, come on, one of the men said. You can't bring a girl like that in here and not stay for a little bit.

The lady wants to go, so we go, Grady said. Tessa, go wait in the car. He handed me the keys.

I went downstairs without him. Goodbye, sweetheart, one of the men said. I sat in the car, shivering. Lit a cigarette from the pack Grady kept in the glove box. I didn't know why I felt so scared, couldn't put my finger on the feeling that was crawling under my skin.

I don't ever want to go back there, I said when he got back in the car a few minutes later.

Jesus, he said. Stop being so uptight.

I mean it. I don't want to.

OK, he said. Fine. Whatever. I don't care.

Thank you.

We drove back in silence. The city disappeared behind us. I watched it go. I was shaking, and I didn't know why.

He dropped me off at my house. Then a strange thing happened. When I was getting ready to get out of the car, he grabbed me by the hair. He kissed the side of my head.

Take care, he said.

OK, I said and went upstairs to bed.

It ended on a day in the spring. I remember it was spring because the leaves were starting to come onto the trees again. Grady had been coming around less. I tracked his absence in my diary, making black marks on the days that he came, leaving blank the days that he did not. I did not tell anyone about this code. I kept it to myself, like everything else about our relationship. If you could even call it that. I called it that. Now I know better.

He came to my house in the middle of the day. It was a Saturday. My mother asked me where I was going. Out, I said. She knew better than to ask me where. I had been disappearing lately, out on my own for walks in the fields or hitching rides with girls from class into town, girls who didn't particularly like me but who wanted even less than I did to be alone. We would wander around the mall, not talking, and then drive back, legs hanging out of the window of their boyfriend's car. Boyfriends, always older. You could get a boyfriend, they always told me. You're alright looking.

I have a boyfriend, I told them.

Who?

He's older, I said. I can't tell you.

They pried me for details. I told them nothing. It was my secret. It felt good to have a secret, kept me warm inside.

But then they would drop me back at my house, and I would be cold again. When Grady's car pulled up in the driveway, I got in without a word. He drove for about five minutes and then pulled off.

I've been seeing someone else, he said.

And you don't want to see me anymore, I finished for him.

Yes, he said.

OK. That's fine then.

Aren't you upset? he asked me.

I don't care, I said, even though I did.

It's not that I don't love you, he said and then didn't finish the sentence.

It's what then?

I don't know, he said.

I looked at his face, really looked at it. It was over. Okay, I said again. I don't care. I drummed my fingers on the armrest of the truck's cab.

He drove me back to my house. He didn't say anything when I got out of the car.

I looked at my face in the mirror. I looked the same as I always had, only different. My face looked harder.

I was in Indianapolis, almost two years later, when it happened. I was in a bar, wearing one of my mother's stolen dresses, when a man came up to me. Tessa, he said.

Why do you know my name? I said.

You're Grady's girl, right?

I was fifteen with a fake ID. I didn't want to be recognized, not when I was half-drunk on martinis and not supposed to be driving my mother's car. I hadn't heard Grady's name in two years and didn't know why this man was talking to me. Slowly it dawned on me. He was one of the men, one of the men from the apartment.

Jesus, he said. You're looking good, girl.

How come you remember my name?

I'm Phil, he said. Suddenly I remembered all of it: their methamphetamine sweat, their beer bellies, the red-rimmed look to their eyes. I recognized him. This is Roger. He gestured to his friend, who looked just like him, only thinner. You're Grady's girlfriend.

I'm not Grady's anything, I said and immediately realized this was the wrong thing to say. Without Grady's protection, I had nothing.

Jesus. You must be some piece of ass, Roger said. Phil told me Grady paid him some pretty penny not to touch you.

What?

He paid us, Phil said. Not to lay a finger on you. You think girls get to just leave Phil's place? He leered at me, and my stomach turned. I don't think so.

Don't worry, honey, we show them a good time.

I have to go, I said and put money down on the table. Too much, but it didn't matter. I wobbled to my car, too drunk to drive, too freaked out, too poor now to call myself a taxi, and with no way to explain anything to my mother. I sat in the car in the parking lot for a long time, wondering if I should call Grady, thank him for saving me from what could have been an untimely end several years ago. But then I realized—I didn't have his number.

I want to say thank you to Grady sometimes. Sometimes I don't know if I know how. Because he took something from me—I'm not sure what. Innocence, maybe. But at the same time I gave it up willingly, or as willingly as I could give it up at that age. And he saved me, in some ways, from giving up parts of myself that I wasn't ready to give up. My ex-fiancé says I'm a cold fish, and maybe I am. Maybe he took something from me that I'll never get back, some kind of emotional core. But I've gotten this far without it, and I don't seem to be missing much.

I think the truth is that nothing is all good or all bad. Lying in the back of that pickup truck, I was the happiest I've ever been. Whiskey in my belly, cigarette smoke in my mouth, Grady's hands on my thighs. Maybe the truth is, I haven't had a happy life. Maybe the truth is, this was all I got. I guess that's a sad thing. I don't know what to make of that.

Inertia

I pretty much stopped being sentimental when Maxwell Kent told me that no, he didn't feel that way about me and that he was sorry for everything that had transpired between us.

What had happened between us was pretty innocent, but it hurt a lot, and I was glad he was sorry.

Kindness is a sort of cruelty, I tell the boy I meet in the kitchen at Lucas's party on Friday night. The boy has flat, glassy eyes and the kind of face that's all angles. I like that. I don't want softness.

How do you mean? the boy asks.

Like, if you're nice to someone, and you don't mean it, I say. That's a kind of cruelty.

I don't know if he understands me, but understanding isn't the point. The point is saying it, putting these things out into the world.

You're strange, is what the boy tells me.

We aren't moving at the same speed or in the same direction. Everyone knows that love exists at the intersection of feasibility and desire. I discovered there was a kind of inertia to it. You could usually tell if it was going to work in the first forty-five seconds. After that you just sat back and waited to collide with the other person.

With Maxwell, I waited and waited, and when it happened, I think we just missed each other. I was too young to read the signs, and that was probably my mistake. We weren't going in the same direction.

I won't go home with you, I tell the boy. He has a bandanna wrapped around his forehead, pinning his bleached hair to his scalp. I like that. I like that kind of scooped-out, hollow personality that affects people who abuse amphetamines.

Sure you won't, the boy says.

He was one of those interesting greasy types that hang around art schools, writing abstract poetry and intense short stories that don't actually go anywhere. Magical realism. There are a lot of these boys. They're easy to pick up at parties because they don't care about anything and a lot of the things they say are accidentally romantic.

I thought I could write a novel about Maxwell, but every time I started, I felt stupid, transcribing all the things that had really happened, but in a gauzy, dreamlike way. The truth was that a lot of the things that had happened felt like a dream—

the way he had waited for me to finish school, leaning against the white wall, or the familiar taste of Evan Williams bourbon in the back of my throat.

I've always been susceptible to beauty. That's how I got into this mess in the first place. There are always beautiful boys hanging around, smiling nastily in the sunlight and tangling your hair in the back.

I give the pages of my novel to the boy.

You're really not bad, the boy says, smearing out his cigarette against the windowsill and tossing the butt in the ashtray. He pauses, considering. What do you do for a living?

What do you mean?

Like, for money, he says. Like, this can't be what pays your bills.

It's not, but I take offense. Why not? I ask. Are you telling me I should keep my day job?

His laugh is loud against the walls of the room, which are bare and white as a dormitory. I can't imagine that a person actually lives here, let alone him. He has notebooks full of poetry in his closet instead of clothing.

Do you want to go somewhere? I ask. We've already had sex and are lying half-dressed in his bed.

Somewhere like where? he says.

Somewhere ends up being coffee and a bagel at a place on the corner with outdoor seating so we can smoke. It's not nice out. The sky is flat and gray, almost colorless.

So, this guy, the boy says. His hair is black where the bleach is growing out. This guy Maxwell. Tell me about him.

Tell me about your ex-girlfriends, I say.

So he's an ex?

It's a little more complicated than that.

I pick the tomato off my bagel. It's Saturday. I hadn't planned on spending the night, but it was late and these things happen. The boy didn't seem to mind that I was still there when he woke up. He queued up a song on the stereo and started getting dressed.

There's a special kind of intimacy, the tenuous kind, that only lasts until you leave, or sometimes not even then. You can tell anything to a stranger.

You can hang out for today, the boy says. If you want. I'm not doing anything important.

Maybe, I say. If I don't think of anything better to do.

We go for an unromantic walk in the park, and the boy tells me about himself. His life story, if you will. Born and raised in Tennessee. Been in love twice. Likes whiskey and loose women. Dislikes talking about himself.

People love talking about themselves, I point out.

In the light his face looks like something different than how I thought it looked in the beginning. I don't know what to make of that. I don't like it when things change, especially people. In the light he is ice: cool, flat cheekbones and a narrow chin. Eyes like blue-black holes. A certain kind of door is closed.

You should let me read your writing, I say.

No.

I don't like things I can't have, I say. I cannot have him. He laughs, his face a paroxysm of moving parts.

I want to talk about it, about Maxwell and the whole long, drawn-out thing, but I don't know where to start. It's the same with the novel. The beginning might as well be the beginning of time. It's not a funny story or a romantic story or even any kind of story at all. I've always admired artists who can make order out of chaos. I just meander along until something sticks.

I want to talk about it, but I don't know if there's anything to talk about. It happened. I look at the trees, which have only just started to have leaves again. The weekend always feels like an empty space.

I could fall in love with you if I wanted to, I say. Like it's easy. Like it's a choice.

You probably could, he says. But you won't.

I don't want to, I say. Because it's true. There is nothing lovable about this boy, no more than anyone else. Soft bodies and grasping hands and eyes and mouths.

Tell me about Maxwell, he says, and I understand it. That he's as much of a voyeur for other people's pain as I am. That he likes watching, cruelly, as other people flounder in the dark.

You're sick, I say. He smiles, slick as a snake. There's no kindness there, only curiosity.

I am an object of curiosity. Sharp and very shiny. Everything goes black around the edges, the sky getting large and looming. Things glitter slightly. The sensation of falling as absolute because I am falling. I smack my head against the ground, and it hurts.

Do you need me to take you home? the boy says. His voice is concerned but very far away.

I wake up in my own bed with the boy in the kitchen, making tea. The kettle whistles. You're awake, good. You passed out pretty much as soon as we got here.

He kneels by the bed, pleased with himself. I got your address off of your driver's license, he says. Your keys were in your pocket. Don't worry, I didn't steal anything.

You didn't have to stay, I manage. Now I might really fall in love with you.

He hands me a mug. You don't want to, he says.

You're right, I say. Are you having fun?

The most fun.

He leaves eventually, but not before leafing through the pages I haven't shown him, the ones that sit in the bottom drawer of my desk. I don't know how he finds them, but he reads all of it, chuckling occasionally to himself. I watch his mouth as it opens and closes, his eyes as they blink and blink again. In the beginning, I liked having another person around. Now I just want him to leave.

This really wasn't such a good idea, I say.

You're probably right, he agrees. One thing, though.

I gather my papers out from under his fingers.

You're not bad, at the writing thing, he says. I think you've got something here. Just try not to be so sentimental about it.

I'm not sentimental.

I'm not going to end up in one of your stories, am I? he asks.

I make a face at him. Good night, I say. Have a nice life.

You know where to find me, he says, and the door shuts behind him.

Maxwell stops by around ten, ten-thirty. I've stopped watching the clock when I hear his knock on the door. I've long stopped expecting him to show up when he says he will, and I'm surprised every time I open the door and his familiar face is waiting there. Hair pushed back over his forehead, new lines around his eyes.

You look older, I say.

Nice to see you too, he says.

It hasn't been that long, not really, but I feel like a different person. I feel like I've shed my skin, and what's left is new and pink and fragile. A few months can do that to a person. I offer him a cigarette, and he takes it. It's good, gives us something to do.

So, he says, after he's fixed himself a drink from the whiskey bottle I keep in the cabinet, next to the macaroni and the iodized salt. Two splashes of whiskey, a little water, and two ice cubes because they're all I have left. I mix my drink with a bottle of cola that's been sitting on the counter for I don't even know how long.

He hasn't taken off his coat, black and heavy around his shoulders. His hair is the color of the sky after it rains, blue tones and yellow gold.

So, I say.

You wanted to talk to me. His voice is solid, real.

I don't know. It's been a while.

That night, that night and the morning after, is on the tip of my tongue. The night where I slept in his bed, the night we slept quiet as fish and chaste as children, staring at the ceiling. In the morning he read the paper, and I imagined that this was how it could be as I sipped black coffee and played with the light that came in through the window. I remember the smell of the newspaper, the fear. I want to know what happened, I say finally. How did this happen?

It happened, he says.

What I don't understand is why it doesn't happen again. That many years of dreaming mean that dreams can take on a life of their own,. Maybe it's me, thinking and not believing, when he tells me the truth of it all. He says it in plain English. I don't feel that way about you, he tells me. His eyes are as serious as the moon.

Tell me what you think, he says.

I think a lot of things, I say. I think it's my fault as much as yours. I think I took too much and you let me, out of obligation or some twisted sense of responsibility. I think I love you, I say. I think we got too close, and it went badly. I think I need to stop thinking about this so much.

Why do you need me to tell you what happened? Maxwell asks. His eyes are as dark as graves. He looks sorry.

I'm sorry too, I say.

He holds my hand. I'm sorry, he doesn't say.

How many times have you been in love? I ask the boy I meet on the dance floor at the party at Lucas's apartment on Friday night. He looks at me, confused, his eyebrows doing a dance of their own. The boy's hands are around my waist.

Too many times, he says. Not enough times.

I laugh. Can I tell you a secret? I ask.

Sure. His voice is low and drawling. I can't remember his name, but his face is like a poem, awful in its construction and desperately sure of itself. In the end their names don't matter.

Everything happens for a reason, I say, and laugh at the mocking of it. I laugh and I sneer and I scare him a little, but not enough that he moves his hands. There's a kind of inertia, waiting for the inevitable. Reassuring.

What's funny? he asks.

I say nothing. I light a cigarette.

Where You End and I Begin

Patrick struggled out of bed around ten, his hands over his eyes. I hadn't slept the night before because he kept kicking me. He stood at the window naked and had a cigarette. I looked at his back, at the bruises that were there, and felt ashamed.

He was not mine to have. Patrick was not anyone's to have, but I had made a mistake.

"Give me a cigarette," I said.

It was a Monday. Normally I would have had to work, but this Monday I didn't. I was supposed to be moving apartments this week. I had taken the time off to move. Last night Patrick had grabbed me by the hip in the hallway. "No," he had said. "Stay."

It was not the first time this had happened. I was always trying to leave, and he was always pulling me back, with his hands and words and magnetic eyes. There was nothing bad about being with him in the dull light of the Halsey apartment, but I knew if I stayed, I would become him. Already I had trouble discerning where he ended and I began.

*

My last boyfriend, Will, was a photographer. He was my first boyfriend in New York. I lived in a studio apartment above a Chinese restaurant, and my walls were always greasy. He constantly told me to stay still, to slow down, to watch the light. It had happened quickly, but somehow he had moved into the apartment, and when we broke up, I needed somewhere to go.

It was fine, I told myself. I hadn't been particularly attached to that apartment anyway.

I hated being with him. I had hated being alone, unmoored, even more. Those first few weeks before school started, I wandered the neighborhood, looking for inspiration. I saw nothing. Gray streets, gray sky, late summer heat, and daylight thunderstorms. Pigeons picked at the scraps left out by the workers in the Chinese restaurant. I had an idea: a young woman, poor and alone in New York, a life shot in high contrast black-and-white. I had imagined myself smoking cigarettes in dimly lit bars and talking existentialist philosophy to men who suddenly understood me. Saying goodbye to my college sweetheart, I had tried to explain it.

He had been heartbroken. I wanted to forget his name. I wanted to stop living my life defined by the varied and inadequate men who always seemed to be stumbling into my apartment half-drunk at four in the afternoon. I hated the city but loved my own space. I made my own time, cooked my meals on a hot plate. Nights I sat alone at bars, which was surprisingly depressing. I took the subway late at night. My college sweetheart wrote bitterly, in an email, that I had watched too many movies.

Life isn't a romance novel, he had told me. But on some level, I didn't believe that.

Warming up soup on my hot plate, working all night, reading, the lights of the city around me. It was large, and it was dirty. Will the photographer had seemed like a good idea at the time. I was lonely, and he had a circle of friends, artsy types with scraggly beards who hung out in the back of restaurants in a self-imposed smoking section, windows flung open, even though there was a chill in the air. *October in Brooklyn*, a note in one of my journals says. The entry is unfinished, dated a week before Halloween. Will would sit on my windowsill with his camera cradled in his hands and tell me to hold still. I disliked this immensely. I disliked him immensely, but I knew no one, and he was somehow plugged in, his eyes trained on a shadow I could understand but not grasp. Once in a while he said something clever and I wrote it down.

This was the sacrifice you have to make, I told myself. This was the life. I worked day and night. Will complained that I didn't sleep. Sleep had become extraneous. I wrote about the dissolution of a relationship and left my journals conspicuously open in public parts of the apartment, hoping he would pick one of them up. In December I slept with someone else.

"You should leave," he told me when I came home in the middle of the night, my lipstick smeared. "I don't want you here anymore."

I wanted to say, this is my apartment. I never wanted you here anyway. And a part of me wanted to fight him, to stay. In between drunken advances and the endless trips to the men's bathroom for more cocaine, more MDMA, more

Ritalin crushed into powder and desperately inhaled, I had touched the *something* I had wanted to touch. I had met people who understood entropy and chaos. I had had several passive discussions about the metaphysical applications of oblivion. Oblivion, of course, was the drug of choice for these people. Whatever could get you closest to the brink, pure passion, pure death. One of Will's friends was obsessed with autoerotic asphyxiation. He was the type who would let slip in casual conversation that he had an erection. In those innocent and childish group situations, where we all slept in the same room, he would be the one whose hands would strangely but unsurprisingly wander, a touch there, a caress here. He came from money.

"It's like, the most intense thing you can imagine," he told me once in his sweet and slightly hoarse voice. He was beautiful, and women threw themselves at him. I could feel Will's eyes on me as he and his friend spoke. Already Will had begun to treat me as if I were a possession, to be won or lost or tossed aside depending on the situation. I leaned closer to this man, whose name was Jack.

"Because when you turn the survival instinct over," Jack was saying, "you find its belly. The instinct that tends toward giving up, toward death."

Jack was the one who stayed up for seventy-two hours to see what kind of hallucinations he could illicit. He had spent a month researching boreholes, which was when you drilled a hole into your skull, hoping to find enlightenment. He would have done it if we hadn't all convinced him it was a terrible idea.

These were the kinds of conversations I wanted. I wanted to live in this world, with all its suspended reality, its complete disregard for the well-being of others. These were not the charitable rich who gave money to starving children in Africa and constantly reminded you, "But what about Haiti?" in casual conversation. These were the hedonists, the padded and protected children of millionaires who were now flexing against their restraints. Humanity without consequence, Jack said once. He was jobless, except that he sold cocaine to his friends at a markup that seemed exorbitant but kept them strung out just enough that he always had customers. And yet sometimes he would disappear for two or three days at a time and reappear with a black eye or a chipped tooth and say nothing about it.

Will was not like the others. Perhaps this was why I disliked him so much. He came from Indiana, which was close enough to my hometown that I felt a kinship. Once in a while he would say something so pleasant and Midwestern that I would have to leave the apartment for several hours to calm down. I had no desire to look backward. I wanted to burn clean of my past and start anew. Already I had started the pathological habit of lying when people asked me where I was from or about my work. At a party for one of Will's friends, a perfectly nice woman had asked me the meaning of the tattoo on my wrist.

The tattoo was of a bird. I had gotten it on a whim when I was eighteen. I did not have and still do not have a very good understanding of object permanence. "Oh, that," I said. "I lost a bet."

I did not explain further. When she asked me what my job was, I told her that I was working on a book of haikus about art and the human condition.

"Oh, I understand," she said after a moment. "You're a nihilist."

Will understood what it meant to work, and it was this that I abhorred. I did not want to work, or at least, I did not want my work to feel like work. I wanted to slide endlessly through my days, stopping to look at something when it glittered, and ultimately continue along, slipping away. I wanted to kill everything that came before and start over.

"Tell me about yourself," he had said when we had met.

"No," I said.

It was Jack who took me in when Will kicked me out in December. It was snowing, and I had very few belongings. When I called him, he was silent for a long time. I had been to his apartment, and I knew he had more than enough room for one small graduate student. I was feeling annoyed and seriously considering leaving the city, quitting school and moving somewhere warm where people didn't know who I was. Since I was young, I always fantasized about getting on a bus or a train and simply disappearing. I wouldn't tell anyone where I was going. With every mile past, I would become less myself and more someone else.

I told this fantasy to only one person, my college sweetheart. His name was Randy, and there was nothing wrong with him except that he was also from Ohio.

"You know it doesn't work like that," he said. "You do know that, right?"

He was from a family of auto mechanics. "What does he know?" I said and shortly afterward decided to move to New York.

But it had become clear that I was not doing well in the city. I wasn't well suited for it.

"You're really a nice girl," Jack said when he rolled open the door to his loft. I stood in the hallway with my two suitcases and wondered if he was going to murder me in cold blood, his hands around my throat. It seemed possible and, at the same time, not entirely disagreeable. I hadn't been doing well in my classes, and besides that, I had no boyfriend, no money, no significant prospects.

"What does that mean?" I said. I hoped to provoke him. He was alone in the apartment, the lights half-on, half-off.

"It means you can sleep on the couch," he told me and stepped aside so I could walk into the apartment.

My old apartment had been dingy, grayish white walls and bad lighting. This apartment was in a nicer part of Brooklyn, high ceilings, low mahogany coffee tables. Jack had been supported financially for many years by an older, wealthy female artist, and their break-up was somewhat legendary. The artist had walked in on Jack hanging suspended from the ceiling by his neck, supported by a silk tie, with one of New York's most well-known and attractive female art dealers stark naked on her knees before him. Everyone involved was so stunned that they nearly forgot to help Jack get down, and he almost died, spending four minutes unconscious. He told me this story that first night. I had already heard the story but not from him. He had spent three nights in the hospital on suicide watch, although he tried relentlessly to explain that it had been an accident. When he got back to the apartment, the female artist had moved out.

"They couldn't take the apartment away from me," he said. "It was in my name, you see."

He seemed particularly smug about that. I hoped very much that I would not have to have sex with him.

"Look," he said. "You're out of your depth. So I'm going to be nice to you."

He put his hand on my knee. "I have a friend who has an apartment out in Bushwick," he said. "And he's looking for a roommate. He's an odd duck, but I bet you can charm him. Okay?"

"Okay," I said.

That was how I met Patrick. The night we met, he broke my nose. There was a party at his house. "Go with me," Jack said. "He'll be in a good mood, and that'll make it more likely that he'll say yes."

Jack approved my outfit, hair, and makeup. He was bisexual, or possibly gay, I realized, and much more interested in women as a means to an end than in any kind of emotional way. This realization made him much less threatening to me. He spoke to me the same way he spoke to everyone, as if they were naked and he was observing, judging. It took some time to get used to, but eventually I learned to live with it. He did these things, made his horrible jokes, simply because no one ever stopped him.

"If someone tells me no," he said once, "I listen."

After I knew that, we were much better friends. We took a car to the Halsey apartment. It was close to the train, but Jack rarely took the subway. He didn't have to take it. People would pay him to go to their parties. Patrick greeted him at the door with a hug and an ostentatious kiss on the mouth.

I was already very drunk myself. Jack had insisted on that. "Patrick doesn't deal with sober people," he told me in the car ride over as we slugged from a plastic bottle of something foul and vaguely reminiscent of high school backseat concoctions: rum and Snapple, vodka and lemonade and Diet Coke. I wanted a cigarette badly.

"Patrick, sweetheart, this is the girl I was telling you about. Who needs the apartment? Her boyfriend kicked her out," Jack said.

"Why's that?" Patrick asked. He had a slight drawl, which I later learned was an affect, not because he hailed from anywhere other than New York. "You were a bad girl, yeah?"

"I don't know about that," I said, shaking a cigarette out of my pack. "My ex was kind of an asshole."

"How so?" Patrick asked me. His eyes had a way of boring into you, like he was looking through you and into the wall behind your back. He was about six feet tall and had sharp black eyes like a bird. He was shirtless, though it was January, and had an army tattoo on one shoulder, a prison tattoo on the other.

"Well, he was kind of boring," I said.

Patrick raised an eyebrow. "Of course," he said. "The ultimate crime." He turned to Jack. "Okay," he said. "Since she comes so highly recommended." He looked back at me. "You can smoke in here. I don't care."

The Halsey apartment was three bedrooms, a large common area with an attached kitchenette, two bathrooms, and a basement. The occupant of the basement was a man named God, who I almost never saw but who sold acid and shrooms and sometimes PCP from the little window of his that looked out onto the street. Patrick lived in the largest bedroom, and a girl named Elisabeth lived in the other one. It was slightly unclear what Elisabeth did, but she wore suits and heels that clicked and was always talking quickly on her phone when she left the house. She was a speed freak and slept only one night out of every three or four, railing lines of coke and speed and sometimes meth in her bedroom, her music low and electronic sounding. Patrick said she was a lawyer or a paralegal or a legal analyst or that she worked on Wall Street. His answer varied depending on when you asked him.

I lived in the smallest room. There were parties every week. There were always people stumbling through, in and out, smoking my cigarettes, looking for drugs, screaming naked through the apartment, lighting things on fire and then putting them out, tossing items out the window, crashing on the couch, making noise in the middle of the night, carving their initials into the walls or tagging mirrors with Magic Markers, having sex in the bathrooms or out on the fire escape, leaving used condoms in the toilet, polishing off bottles of wine on Thursday nights, killing a thirty-two rack of Budweiser on Fridays, taking one too many Klonopin and then tripping down the stairs and breaking an arm or possibly a leg. Patrick broke my nose by accident, his elbow popping back to uncork a bottle of wine. As the blood poured down, he apologized profusely, slurring, and said he would knock a hundred dollars off my rent.

We went to the emergency room that first night, and Jack got lost somewhere. Patrick kissed me in the back of the taxi. It hurt like a sonofabitch. My nose exploded with pain, and I knew I had to move in with him. "You look beautiful with those black eyes," he said.

"You're crazy," I said. But crazy was what I had been looking for, although it had another name: passion. I wanted fire. I wanted, suddenly and horribly, the Halsey apartment, where nights never ended and we spent our days dazed, lying stoned on the couch at three in the morning, watching the stars through the ceiling.

My nose never healed straight. January came and went. Early mornings, watching the light creep up and over the windowsill, I would watch Patrick sleep. He slept like the dead, on his back, hair a sunburst on the pillow. Elisabeth would come into his room like they were siblings, like she didn't mind his nakedness, his disarray. I never got used to that.

I moved my things into my own room, but almost every night I ended up in his bed, his hands pressing into me. I felt like dough. He left imprints. He would be sitting on the sofa swigging from a whiskey bottle when I came home from class or work, shirtless, cigarette between his lips. I wanted to get used to him, but I never could. He set my nerves on edge.

He was a politics student originally, and his room was piled high with books, textbooks mostly, stolen from used bookstores all over the city. Most of them still had the yellow "used" stickers on the spine, panicked notations from frantic students in the margins. Most of it was unintelligible. He had books on abnormal and criminal psychology and piles of notebooks full of notes. Unlike me, who was working toward a degree, Patrick seemed simply to be studying for the sake of studying. He had no major overarching questions about the nature of humanity that he longed to answer. He had no research point of view. He occasionally was called by a friend of his to teach a class at a local community college. Later he made a scene, after some bad acid, and was not asked back.

He was twenty-eight but looked twenty. There was a kinesthesia about him, a frenetic, manic quality, which only slowed when he slept. It was as if his molecules were simply vibrating too quickly for him to show any signs of aging or slowing down. He would wake up in the mornings and work, scribbling maniacally in one of his notebooks (or, sometimes, in one of mine) until it was dark out. Or he wouldn't wake up at all, or spend the day in bed, smoking my Parliaments and drinking a lukewarm Corona from a twenty-four-ounce glass bottle.

He hadn't ever had to grow up, and this fascinated me. The days I had to teach, I put on my one nice blazer and carried a beat-up briefcase. They gave me starter classes: introductions, 101s. I was desperately unqualified. I would come home exhausted and nervous, and Patrick would ignore me until I calmed down. He would make a couple of phone calls, and people would appear. We would sit around the living room in a circle and talk about nothing until the day had melted away into blackness.

There were nights when he wasn't with me. There were nights when I didn't want him or when I found myself kissing a stranger in a black room, struggling to pull my shoes off or unbuckle a belt, hands grabbing, teeth gripping, the walls a terrible smear. We never spoke about these nights.

"I don't own you," he told me once and stroked my hair like I was a cat.

One Friday Jack came over. It had been several months since I had seen him. I had seen Will two or three times at parties, and he had avoided eye contact. He had someone else now, a girl who looked very young, photogenic—all clear skin and bright eyes. I hoped she was able to stay still enough for him.

Jack, on the other hand, made a beeline for me. I was standing by the window. He looked tired. He was in his thirties and looked it. The smell of cigarettes followed him like a halo. I later learned that his inheritance money had finally run out, and he had been supporting himself selling drugs, taking new risks. Evidently it had worn on him.

"How are you?" I said.

He grimaced and didn't answer. "How are you?"

"I'm really good," I said. It was half-true. The days had begun to blur together into a sickening stretch, but I was working. There was Patrick, like a shooting star, on all the time, around me. He lounged, paging through a book, smoking my Parliaments or his Camel Straights, or he stayed up late and we talked through my thesis, through his work, or we did lines of speed off the back of a magazine and fucked, clinging to one another, until the sun came up behind us like a bad surprise.

Jack looked ill. "You look all right. I had heard you weren't doing so well here."

"Why?" I gripped the neck of my wineglass.

"Well, I know what Patrick is like," he said. I tried to remember the time when I thought Jack was kindly, hiding behind his bawdy talk and the rope burns on his neck. Now I saw he was a dirty old man, defined only by his desires, by his wants.

Later I would think about that. We were all defined like that. Sweaty, panicked children. It was June, God, and then it was July. Time was sick, and it dripped off the walls like acid. I finished my first year of school and was promptly told by the program director that my work had raised some red flags. My professors had circled words and phrases on my final papers, saying, "All right, you've gone too far here."

I didn't know what too far felt like. I felt like I was exactly where I wanted to be, tumbling into half-sleep in the early afternoons, Patrick's arm heavy around me.

My scholarships were in jeopardy. "You have talent," they were saying, "but sometimes talent isn't enough." I tried to remember why I had hated the city when I had moved in, nearly a year before. I barely remembered the apartment that Will had taken from me. It left an impression of white walls scrubbed hard, dusty wooden floors, bad light. I had notes in my notebooks, that was all.

It happened slowly, and then all at once. They call it collective hysteria. Elisabeth was staying up nights with me, chattering maniacally, editing proofs with a red pen in one hand and a wine glass in her other hand. Constantly smoking like a chimney. She would sit with her blouse unbuttoned, her bra exposed, pencil skirt askew. She looked like a bad movie. Bad nights, God would emerge from the basement in a haze of marijuana, or occasionally hashish, and bring with him obscure references to philosophers and small baggies of little white pills. People doing yard work kept me awake when I tried to sleep in the mornings. Summer was a thought.

When I tried to remember what spring had felt like, it was gone. It had burned off, I think, in the mad dash to prepare for summer. Summer was the main event. I had moved to New York in early September, missing the first week of classes. That was when I had been able to find an apartment, and I was sure my professors had held it against me. "You don't need school," Patrick whispered to me in the hallway on a long Friday before he disappeared into the bathroom with a girl I didn't recognize. I ended up letting an undergraduate Journalism major push me onto the mattress in Elisabeth's bedroom. Instead of changing the sheets, we threw them out the window. The journalism major looked like he had won the lottery.

Leaves on the trees, one of my notebooks read. The entry was dated sometime in June. *Where did they come from?*

I paid my rent in cash on the first of the month. God sputtered something obscure and then retreated downstairs. He had a girlfriend, a redhead who came and went like smoke.

I had hated the city. Now it was a way of being. Patrick with his red-blond hair and black eyes, the army tattoo on his shoulder. He had not gone into the army, but his brothers had, and they brought home army-made tattoo machines: a ballpoint pen rigged up to I don't know what. I had an image in my head of Patrick at seventeen, teeth gritted, as one of his brothers—they were only an impression, a red-blond succession of men who looked like Patrick and yet were fundamentally different—pressed a needle repeatedly into his skin. It was his brothers' army insignia, scarred into his shoulder. He carried his family with him everywhere.

He seemed to be from nowhere. He was too old to act like this, but he did anyway. He was not from nowhere; he was from New Jersey, from a blue-collar working-class family. One of his brothers was dead. His father was in prison, doing fifteen-to-life for killing Patrick's stepmother.

"She was a bitch," Patrick said.

His father was not a good man. He had been dishonorably discharged from the army for something suspect, something nasty, unspeakable. I never met him. The other brothers had left home as quickly as possible, three of them to the army and one on a mathematics scholarship. Ironically, the one on scholarship was the dead one. "Amphetamine overdose," Patrick told me. I had learned to doubt the things he said. The army brothers were scattered, but they kept in touch. They had returned to give him the tattoos. Patrick had gone to his oldest brother's wedding, and now there were reddish blond children running around in a house somewhere in Camden, Jersey, children Patrick had met only once or twice and rarely spoke about.

Patrick's father was somewhere upstate. The first Sunday of every month, Patrick got up at four in the morning to catch a bus and visit him. "He's not a good man," Patrick said often when people asked about his family. "But someone has to visit him."

Patrick was the load-bearer. At fifteen, when his last brother had split, he had stayed with the old man and made sure he didn't die in his sleep, asphyxiated on his own whiskey vomit. Patrick still had the cigarette burn scars. After his father had passed out, Patrick would pour the last of the whiskey from his father's glass on his new wounds to disinfect them and then finish off the bottle, smoking the last of his father's cigarettes.

I got used to him being gone that first Sunday. Later I got used to him being gone period.

He went to the prison to remind himself: Don't be like that. I felt it was the same as if I had made a monthly pilgrimage back to Ohio to see my mother rotting in her suburban home, my father half-dead from working long shifts and his diabetes, my sister with too many children. In a dying city with no light.

But I made no such pilgrimage, and Patrick did. He felt no sympathy for the dead stepmother, who Patrick's father had married after Patrick was long gone, disappeared into the bowels of New York City. It is remarkable the violence we can suffer and still survive. "She chose to be with him," Patrick said. "I was just born. It's different."

When he visited his father now, he did so from behind a thin sheet of bulletproof glass.

The Sunday before that Monday, the last Monday, Patrick had gone to visit his father. When he returned, he was like he always was after a visit, grabbing me, grabbing at me, forcing me to drop whatever work I had been trying to do. It was September now. He was alive, and I was barely making it to classes, hungover or still drunk, trembling from a weird concoction of drugs. It happened slowly. I had been plotting my escape.

"I'm just not cut out for this," I told Elisabeth, who nodded. Knowingly. She was cut out for it; in fact, she needed the speed, which would have made other people afraid. She needed to feel her lips peel back from her face and wait for the adrenaline drop, the first turn on the roller coaster over and over again. You could bottle that feeling and sell it. I wished I could bottle Patrick and take a dose of him whenever I needed one, but the truth was that I didn't need him. I didn't need him the way I hadn't needed Will, and before him, who else? There was always an else. I needed nothing. I needed a cigarette, a cup of weak coffee, I needed to do the forty pages of reading before Thursday, I needed to get out of here.

"Some people can't do this," Elisabeth said. "You shouldn't feel ashamed of it." But in her eyes there was pity and, beneath that, survivor's envy. It would have been so much easier, her eyes said, if she could make the choice I was making.

I had found God, and he lived in a basement in Bushwick.

I was not his to have. I did what I had to do. When they put me in the hospital, I tried to explain it. Patrick came and visited me behind the glass. I told him I didn't want to see him anymore. The stitches in my wrists hurt like a sonofabitch. "Take your time," the scholarship people had said, but I could tell they were tired of me. They wished there had been more warning signs, that they could have cut the limb off the tree before the rot spread.

Jack never said anything else to me. I was not his to have.

Listen to me, I told the orderlies. They ignored me.

They call it collective hysteria. Some poison crept into my blood. I became the load-bearer. I was not afraid. I had to leave, and then I did.

Trying to Escape the Inevitable

June has this recurring dream. They're talking, she and Dennis, and it's going great, everything is wonderful, and then she has to leave for a minute, just go grab something from somewhere, and when she comes back, he's gone. Just gone. She spends the rest of the dream looking for him, and when she wakes up, she has the taste of metal in her mouth, and she's alone in bed.

June's favorite band growing up was from Detroit, and that's where Dennis is from. She wanted to go see them when she was sixteen, and her mother said: Hell, no. Her mother was probably right. June thinks about that sometimes. Dennis wasn't even in Detroit by then. He had already moved to Brooklyn.

June grew up in a studio apartment on Twenty-Third Street. Everyone always says, wow, you grew up in Chelsea, you must be loaded, but really they were rent-stabilized, and she went to public school. She wanted to change schools and go to private school like her best friend, Melissa, but her mom was like: Don't even think about it. Her mother was probably right about that too. When you get older you start to realize that your parents aren't actually as dumb as you think.

When June told her mother she was getting married, her mother said: Why? Her mother has been married three times, twice to June's father, and she thinks the whole thing is a crock of shit. June tends to believe her. But she tells her mother: Dennis asked, and I said yes, and we're going to go through with it. I don't know why you would do such a thing, her mother shouts from the kitchen, while June sits on the couch in the living room. Her mother is still there in the apartment on Twenty-Third Street with no husband and no kids and only the cat to keep her company.

I'm doing it because we're in love, Ma, June says.

Love, her mother says and laughs, and keeps making coffee.

That night June tells Dennis what her mother said. His own parents aren't coming for the wedding—they can't stand each other, and besides, they live in Florida and Belize; it would be too expensive. June has met his mother once. She pinched June's cheeks and told her she was too good for her son, but she also kept getting Dennis confused with his older brother, the one who does drugs. His father, apparently, isn't much fun either, but June would like to meet him before she ties herself to Dennis forever.

Nothing is forever, Dennis tells her.

Even if we die, we'll still be married, June says.

No, we won't, he says. We'll just be dead. Then he rolls over and goes to sleep.

*

Dennis is fourteen years older than June, but they try to pretend it doesn't matter. When he was sixteen, she was two years old. She thinks about that sometimes.

When he was smoking his first joint, she was in diapers.

When he was kissing his first girl, she was learning the alphabet.

When he was losing his virginity, she was getting potty-trained.

He's older, an established writer, with two books out and a novel in the works, which makes June feel like she doesn't know what she's doing. She's just a journalism student. At Columbia, but still. She knows he could get her a job at *The New York Times* if she asked, but she doesn't want to ask. He never wants to talk about work. He has tattoos up and down his arms, but he's never told her what they mean, and she's never asked.

On the Tuesday before the wedding, they go to the movies. Two adults for *Spider-Man,* Dennis tells the ticket-taker, who flirts with him even though June is standing right there. She's pissy all the way up the stairs.

What did I do this time? he asks.

The ticket girl was totally flirting with you, and you didn't even notice.

You're mad at me because I *didn't* notice someone was flirting with me? Jesus.

We're getting married in six days. I should think you would notice—I don't know.

You're being ridiculous.

In the theater, June can't focus on the movie. All she can think about is that the ticket-taker is probably ten years younger than she is, and one of these days, Dennis is going to find someone younger and cuter than she is, and she'll be replaced. She knows because she replaced the one who came before her.

We're getting married, she tells herself.

Somehow, that doesn't seem like enough.

Dennis was June's best friend from college's roommate after she moved out of her ex-boyfriend's apartment. It's a lot of degrees of separation, but that's how they met. June was just always around, and one night he came out with them, and she got way too into talking about the past tense, and he thought it was cute, her passion for the intricacies of grammar, and he was a writer himself, and he asked her if she wanted to come home with him. In the morning, she texted her friend and told her what had happened.

Nice, her friend said. I knew you two would get along.

Since then, they've broken up twice, gotten back together twice. June doesn't know what it is about him. He's so—unremarkable. He's got stupid hair and crooked teeth, and he doesn't smoke cigarettes, so she's stopped smoking too, which she hates. She's become one of those quitting-smoking people. He makes her crazy. He's all she can think about, even now, after years. It's very frustrating. She wishes she could focus on something else.

June's mother helps her with her hair and makeup on the day of. You look beautiful, she says. Too bad this won't last.

Don't say things like that, Ma.

What? It's the truth. The women in this family have bad luck.

June's dress isn't white. It felt disingenuous. June and Dennis have been living together for two years already. The dress is blue, scoop neck, midlength. It's nice.

The ceremony itself doesn't take that long. June's friends and Dennis's friends are there, her mom, a couple of cousins on her mom's side.

Dennis looks cute in his suit, cute and uncomfortable. His vows are short and sweet.

I don't know why I'm doing this, but I said I would, and I know I love you, so here we go.

Right, June says.

After, they have a reception. Everyone gets drunk. I guess we're married now, June tells Dennis.

I guess we are.

Funny, June says. I don't feel any different.

June has this recurring dream. She and Dennis are at a fast-food restaurant, only he's serving her, and she's a customer. He suddenly starts being mean to her. She never remembers what he says, but he says horrible things, and she starts to cry. Why are you saying all these horrible things? she asks him.

Because you deserve them.

June always wakes up crying.

What's wrong? Dennis will say. He will extend his arms open wide and wrap her up in them like a papoose. Shh, he will say. Go back to sleep.

And June goes back to sleep.

Pursuit

Beauty is one of those things. "What do you do?" Red asked. I was nineteen, drunk in a bar, and I couldn't tell the truth.

"I'm a curator," I lied.

"So you decide what art goes where?"

"No," I said, and now I was telling the truth. "I look for beauty, and I collect it when I find it."

"Is that why you're talking to me?" There was a sardonic flicker around his mouth. I returned it with a smile of my own.

"Beauty is cruelty," I said. He understood what I meant.

He was as pretty as a picture, but I was tired of boys, even the pretty ones. With their hands and eyes and arms, and the way they always wanted something. I didn't mind giving it to them, but when I was eighteen, I didn't know any better, and now I was almost twenty. I had my feet under me a little bit more. Still, when he slid over to me with his eyes and hands and arms and bought me drink after drink, I let him.

Eventually I had to leave him because he made me feel like I was shrink-wrapped, like all the air had gone out of the room. That's a sensation one can only tolerate for short, attractive bursts of time. His phone number was in my pocket, but I wasn't going to call.

In the morning I was tired, tired of talking to people and having to express myself with a tool as inelegant as language. Words are so tiresome, so clunky, especially late at night and after a few drinks. I was almost disgusted by the thick layer of poetry that had left a residue on my tongue. I am not a great lover of literature.

He was waiting for me when I got to work in the morning, a grin stretched nastily across his face. "What do you want?" I said. I was hungover, annoyed.

"I love you," he said. "I want to marry you. Let's run off to the country and raise children and goats." There was a cigarette tucked behind his ear. "Have you ever had goat's milk? It's incredible."

I went to the espresso machine, which hadn't been cleaned, and made myself an Americano. Waitressing is not a romantic job. It's not romantic in the grit that accumulates behind the coffee machine or the grease that lines the inside of the counter where the sponges don't reach. Still, I could see him painting a picture in his head, a picture of me as the nineteen-year-old waitress and art student, struggling to make ends meet and picking up boys in bars, hoping that one day someone would rescue her from her tortured (but ultimately poetic) existence. He was the type of boy who did things like that.

I was not in the mood to be rescued. For that, I would have had to be slightly stoned and wearing much more comfortable shoes. No one ever runs away from their problems in an apron with their name embroidered on the front. "No," I said shortly and sipped my coffee in a way that let him know I was finished with the conversation. He was crestfallen, slightly. It was sweet, the way puppies are sweet. Suddenly I didn't want to see him, didn't want to remember him touching me. "That's enough of that," I said and shooed him out of the diner with a damp rag and my indifference.

Cal came in around closing and leaned on the counter. "Mary Ann," he said, for that was the name I was using in those days, "you really need to learn how to connect with people. A good waitress is personable."

I poured him a black coffee. Cal was unemployed. He was utterly unsuited for labor of any kind. Some family member sent him checks every month, not a lot, but enough to live on, some kind of trust fund, and he never seemed to mind being broke all the time. "I'm not a waitress," I said. "I'm an art student."

"You say that," he said, "but I've never actually seen you draw anything."

I reminded him of the charcoal sketches from life drawing class, the still-life paintings, the sketches on napkins of customers who stayed particularly still.

"That's not art," he said. "You do it for class or because you're bored. I want to see what you make on your own time."

"Art school is more of a conceptual experience," I said. Cal gritted his teeth, took a drink from his coffee, and said he was going out for a cigarette. Cal was always going out for a cigarette or coming back from having a cigarette or thinking about having a cigarette. He had been fired from his last job for excessive smoke breaks.

Everyone had theories about my art, not just Cal. When Angela and Janice came in twenty or thirty minutes later, they were full of conspiratorial notions about the art world, about the regular world, about everything. Angela was a heinous tweaker who occasionally said insightful things, and Janice followed her around, writing them down. Janice swore that Angela would be famous someday. They were in love, but it was a tactful, perfunctory sort of love, more of a business agreement than a passionate one.

Last to arrive at the diner was Timmy. They all gathered at a booth in the back, near a window so Cal could smoke and Timmy could roll a joint, or so they could pass around a small amber pill bottle, unmarked. Once in a while a legitimate customer would come in, sneer at them, and order a BLT, plus coffee, black. Anyone who hangs out at a diner after 10 p.m. is not to be trusted.

It was around midnight when I finished, and after Artie, the night manager, had locked up and gone home to his wide wife and vaguely sticky children, there was some talk of going to the bar. I was feeling stretched out and sick, but as usual my friends were irrepressible.

It was no surprise, unfortunately, that he was back at the bar, nursing something in a draft glass.

"Do you know that guy?" Angela asked me over the rim of her wiry glasses. "He looks like he knows you."

"One of your various affections?" Cal asked. He had the capacity to be nasty and often used it. "Or affectations, I might say. He's pretty."

"They're always pretty," Janice said in a lofty way that didn't mask her jealousy. "Mary Ann likes pretty."

"Everyone likes pretty," I said. There was a drink in front of me, a gin and tonic, and I wasn't entirely sure how it had gotten there.

"What's his name?" Angela asked.

"No comment." This brought a round of laughter to the group.

He caught me by the hip a little later, as I was walking toward the bathroom. "Can I come with you?" he asked.

His name was Red, and we exchanged pleasantries as we walked to his apartment around two in the morning, under the heavy blanket of the sky. There was a bottle of whiskey in his apartment; that was the pretense, but the pretense was the pretense. I was not drunk, but there was a beery cast to the way he was moving, which made me feel like I was more in control of the situation then I was.

"I'm not in love with you," he said in the flat, toneless way that people speak when they've done too many amphetamines. "I was bored, I didn't sleep. I wanted to see you again."

"I didn't think you were," I said. I was a little pleased I had made such an impression. "People don't fall in love over the course of one night."

"Do you speak from experience?" he asked. We turned off the avenue and onto a side street, tree-lined and dark except for the buzzy orange of the streetlamps. "How many times have you been in love?"

I ran a hand through my hair, fingers catching in the knots. Last time we had gone to my apartment, and he had been gone when I woke up. I liked it when they were gone by the time I woke up.

"Three times," I said honestly, or honestly enough.

"And how did those go for you?" He stopped in front of a building made of red bricks and green paint. "This is me."

"Nice building," I said, ignoring the question.

"So they went badly," he said, slightly smug. We walked up the stairs.

"Why 'Red'?" I asked, sprawled out under his sheets.

"Why not?"

"It's such an obvious nickname," I said. I watched the smooth line of his throat as he dragged on his cigarette.

"What's wrong with my name?" he said. "Why Mary Ann? You're not exactly a sitcom character."

"Names are funny," I said.

"A lot of things are funny," he said.

Timmy picked me up for class on Monday. Timmy was from down South, a tiny town north of Atlanta, and he refused to relinquish his pickup truck, even though it was a constant struggle to find parking. He was judicious about handing out rides, but we lived only a few blocks from one another, and I had my enormous portfolio bag to lug around.

"Whatever happened with that guy?" he asked as soon I was settled in the cab. Timmy spoke infrequently, but he was relentless when it came to other people's personal business.

"What do you mean, whatever happened?" I asked and snatched the pack of cigarettes that was resting on the dashboard.

"I mean, you disappeared," Timmy said, snatching his cigarettes back. "With mysterious-bar-guy. Leather-jacket-wearing, fancy-drink-drinking guy. Whose name is?"

"Not important," I said. "Maybe I should ask you about your latest exploits."

Timmy's Irish face turned scarlet. "That's all right, thank you," he said, pulling the truck out of its parking space. It was only a twenty-minute drive to school, but it took an hour on the train. "He seemed nice."

"I wouldn't say nice," I said.

"Well, who wants nice?" he said. "You do like pretty, shiny things."

"I do," I said.

He didn't pry further. Friends know when to ask and when to shut up. Instead, he prattled on about which model he thought we'd have today and the relative merits of Marilyn versus Erica, or Kenneth versus Michael. All the models were on a regular rotation, so we got to know them personally, chatting between poses. It's easier to stare at a naked person for six hours at a stretch when you know you can chat politics with them during break.

My favorite was Marilyn. Marilyn was not beautiful. The most beautiful of the models was a slim Asian girl named Carla who had long hair that moved down her back in waves and a sinuous way of moving that allowed her to make graceful shapes. But she had trouble getting back into long poses and shivered almost imperceptibly, which made her difficult to draw. Marilyn was a professional, although her body was awkward with heavy breasts and long, strange legs. She was interesting. There was something important about that.

Not everything could always be beautiful, I thought as we pulled into a fortuitous parking spot directly in front of the fine arts building. There had to be contrast.

Red was outside, grinning, leaning against a motorcycle that wasn't his when I walked out. Angela was walking next to me, and she grabbed my shoulder as we passed the security guards. "Isn't that the guy?" she said. I had no idea what she was talking about until I saw him.

"Hey," he said. Angela ceased to be important. She said a hasty goodbye and rushed off.

"What are you doing here?" I asked. "Since when do you drive a motorcycle?"

"I don't," he said. "I just thought it looked cool. Like an old movie. James Dean and all that."

"You're an idiot."

He shrugged, a fluid motion that distracted me for a moment. "Yeah," he agreed easily. "That's fair."

"Why are you here?"

"Why not?" he said. "I thought I'd take you to lunch."

"We're seeing an awful lot of each other, aren't we?" I started walking, and as I expected, he fell into step behind me.

In the daylight he looked different, brighter, with a translucence to his skin that I hadn't noticed before. He wore a dark blue denim jacket and black jeans, and his black T-shirt was clean but faded. He smelled like smoke and denim.

"I suppose so," he said.

There was something pleasing, something refreshing, about the careless way he spoke to me. I knew I couldn't hurt him; he was untouchable. He stared at me as if through a pane of glass. I liked the pane of glass. Through it, everything had a sort of irony and light.

"So you're on your way to being a curator?" he asked over a cup of weak coffee in a small coffee shop I had never been to before. We had walked and walked, talking about art mostly, before he gestured to a blue-and-white awning. "Best chocolate croissants in the city," he said. "But terrible coffee."

Calling it coffee was a stretch. It was more like coffee-flavored water. The croissant, however, was incredible, and I was considering ordering a second one.

"Sort of," I said. "I think I'd like it, and I think I'd be good at it. I already curate so much of my life."

"You do have a bit of a thing with control," he said. There was a flicker in his eye as he said, "Why do school at all, if you know what you want to do?"

"I like to draw," I said. "It's a luxury, being allowed to do something you like all day. I won't always have that."

"And it's worth working nights and weekends, being tired all the time?" He took a sip of his coffee, wrinkled his nose. "It seems like a lot of work, that's all."

"Well, it's got to be better than the alternative."

Setting sunlight slanted in through the window, and it lit up his hair like a halo around his face. "The alternative?"

"Getting some menial office job, slaving away, dying alone."

"I guess that's boring, maybe," he said. "But it pays the bills. And I have time for myself."

"To do what?"

"Oh, you know," he said. "Loaf around."

Loafing, it turned out, was what he did. When I started to snoop around his apartment later, I found strong evidence that he was a loafer. There were almost a hundred boxes of macaroni in the cupboards, stacked up neatly like puzzle pieces. It looked like that was the only food he owned, that and some instant coffee, a little old milk, and some salt and pepper.

There were some books. Actually, a lot of books. It seemed like every corner I turned, there were more books—in shelves and stuffed into milk crates, cardboard boxes and even in stacks, haphazardly arranged wherever there was room. He lived alone. His apartment was just a bedroom, bathroom, and kitchen. The books, when I examined them, seemed to have no rhyme or reason. There were just as many trashy airport mystery novels as there were works of classic Western literature.

The most interesting thing I found in the entire apartment was a bin of old notebooks full of Red's scribbling handwriting. There were poems in there and what seemed like pieces of short stories, descriptions of people, and even little sketches to accompany them. I was deeply involved in one of the notebooks when I heard the key in the lock. I dropped it to the floor and got back in bed.

Red held a carton of eggs in one hand and a single onion in the other. "I got breakfast," he said.

I pretended to be half-asleep. It was past noon. "That's breakfast?"

"When I cook it, yes." He put the eggs down on the kitchen counter. The apartment was small enough that he could see me from the door. "You were looking through my things."

I sat up, reached for a cigarette. "I just wanted to get to know you," I said. It sounded like a lie even as I said it.

He laughed, a harsh sound. "Shut up and eat your eggs," he said. "You'll have to get to know me the normal way, through time spent together and deep conversation."

He put a pan on the stove and turned on the burners. "That's okay," he said. "Who wants to get to know each other anyway? Let's do this instead."

This turned out to be breakfast, a midday nap, watching some movies in bed, and screwing around before falling back asleep. We didn't talk about ourselves, our lives, our goals, all the things that people talk about when they first meet. We'd talked about those things, and we didn't want to know any more about one another. All I wanted to know about him was the way he fell asleep, the way he smoked a cigarette, the way he thumbed through a book of essays when he thought I wasn't looking.

We fell in love like that, when no one was looking, neither of us trying or realizing until it had already happened. It wasn't particularly pleasant, as experiences go. But it happened.

Time passed in a trickle, then in a stream. There were no great romantic moments, no dramatic music swells. There was waking up in the morning and turning over to find Red smoking a cigarette and waiting to tell me about his dreams. There was going out to the bar and the way he made all my friends laugh, so much that even Cal did a spit take into his glass of overpriced beer. There was walking twenty-five minutes in the cold and coming home to a warm bed. He had a cat sometimes, an orange tabby that came and went from the window in his room that led to the fire escape. We named it Marmalade.

"So what's going on with your boy?" Cal asked me late at night at the diner. He was in the middle of a period of existentialist dread. "You two seem pretty chummy."

I knew he was only asking because he was trying to distract himself. He was coming off a week-long binge of *something*, and it was making him jumpy and overwhelmed by the world.

"I guess we're all right," I said. No one else was in the diner; all the customers were gone, and the rest of our friends had gone to see a concert somewhere downtown earlier in the evening. Cal didn't like crowds, and he rarely went to those kinds of events, even if everyone else was going.

"I'm just saying," he said, running a hand through his greasy hair. "I've never seen you like this before. Not that anyone else would notice," he confirmed. "Unless they knew you really well."

"And you know me really well?"

"Of course." Cal smirked. "You're looser. You're getting soft, Mary. It's a little embarrassing."

I picked up his empty coffee cup. "Are you finished with this?"

"I don't mean it in a bad way," he said, nodding for me to take the cup away. "I'm just telling you because I don't think you realize what you're doing. You used to be really interesting, you know? With your collections and all that. You used to be ruthless. Now you're just like everyone else. Another girl falls in love and ruins her potential."

"What makes you the king of the universe? Why do you get to decide who is interesting and who isn't?"

Cal smiled a greasy smile. "Everyone has their truth," he said simply. "Everyone has that thing they're looking for. This is mine."

"You should leave," I said quietly. "I have to close up, and I don't want to look at your face anymore."

He nodded. "You're weak now, Mary Ann."

"Get out."

I busied myself with closing the diner, playing the music loud enough that I couldn't hear Cal's words in my head. Red was due to pick me up any minute, but I wasn't sure I wanted to see his face either.

"Am I weak?" I asked when he showed up riding a spindly blue frame bicycle, twenty minutes after he had said he would be there. "Like, do you think that us being together has made me less interesting?"

Red laughed. "Definitely," he said. "People are always less interesting when you really get to know them."

"So what, everything has an expiration date?" I said. "When it just gets so boring that you can't stand it anymore?"

"Yep," he said, and then I got on the handlebars of the bike, and we rode away.

He was as pretty as a picture, and I painted him in oils and sold it to a predatory gallery owner who preyed on art students who were willing to sell paintings for little more than the cost of materials. "I like your work," the gallery owner said in a cheap, flimsy way that made me think it was part of some kind of rehearsed speech. "Make me ten more like this, and maybe we can talk about a little show."

I knew the kind of shows that art students got. They were small, poorly attended, and you could bet that the gallery would take such a cut that I wouldn't make any money. But I had all these paintings of Red taking up space in my apartment. It was better to sell them for nearly nothing than to keep them for nothing at all.

"You're making money off of me," Red said, sprawled in bed as I sketched out my next painting in charcoal on a canvas panel. "I should get a cut."

"You'll reap the benefits of my eternal gratitude," I said. Red's face was difficult to draw, as most beautiful faces are. Symmetry is hard to replicate. I was concentrating, and his talking was making it difficult.

"What is it with you and my face?" he asked. He asked this question frequently. "Why do you like it so much?"

"Why do you like my face?" I countered.

"It's nice," he said. I am no great beauty. "I like your nose. I like the way your mouth moves when you talk."

"I'm not pretty," I said. "Not in the easy way. You know that."

"Pretty's overrated."

"You can say that because you've got it." I traced the curve of his jaw with my charcoal pencil and then rubbed it out with my thumb. "It's like currency. When you're rich, you don't think about money anywhere as much as when you're poor."

"You're not poor," he said.

"Maybe upper middle class," I said. "You can come to my gallery opening when I'm rich and famous. Be my trophy boyfriend."

He held out a hand, and I shook it. "Deal."

Summer came with all of its terrible heat. Janice went back to San Fran, and Angela was house sitting for a family in Long Island, which mostly meant that she lounged on the beach all day and sent me long emails telling me to visit. Timmy had hit some sort of depression and disappeared into the goth clubs in the Lower East Side, spiking his blond hair and ringing his eyes in eyeliner. Occasionally I saw him at the bar, but he was taking a much-needed break from civilized society, and I respected that.

The only person I saw was Cal, and that was because he insisted on lurking around. I did have a gallery opening, a very small one, in May, which was lightly attended, and I managed to sell two more paintings. Red sold a short story, which was a big deal because he hadn't sold anything in more than three years. We lived well, for a time, drinking a bottle of red wine every night.

Cal sneered when he passed me on the street, which was frequently; he knew where I lived, and besides, we went to a lot of the same parties. Before the semester ended, Angela and Janice had expressed their desire to distance themselves from him.

"He's just getting so dark," Angela had said. His particular brand of grumbling was at odds with her sunny cynicism. "He's mean, Mary. He's really nasty nowadays."

We only had one year of school left, and everyone figured it was easier to ignore Cal than try to change him. He would, likely enough, end up slinking into one dark corner of the city or another after graduation. His photography had a gritty, seedy look that appealed to lots of magazines, and he would make a living feeding off the subculture that he seemed to deride the most. Red summed it up the best over dinner on an extremely humid August evening.

"I hate that guy," he said, "but he'll be more successful than any of us because he has no soul."

The end, like the beginning, happened suddenly. Red stood in the doorway of my apartment in early September, and I knew. "You're leaving," I said.

"Everyone is always leaving," he said. He meant it as a joke, but I knew what he meant. He was wearing a suit and tie, and he looked like something out of an old movie for a second, before the veil was lifted and he was himself again. "I have to see a man about a funeral."

"That doesn't mean you don't have to come back," I said.

"I know," he said, nodding. He picked up an empty pack of cigarettes from the table by my doorway and turned it over in his hands.

"But you're not coming back."

"I really can't say." He paused. "We're a little too comfortable here, don't you think?"

"What do you mean?"

"I mean, we've relaxed." He said it like a dirty word, and I heard echoes of Cal's nastiness in his tone. "It's not a bad thing necessarily. But I've been feeling restless."

I knew that. I had noticed over the past month the way he didn't sleep anymore. If I woke up in the middle of the night, chances were he was up, sitting by the window, smoking and looking at the moon, or paging through some book with the cover obscured by his palm. "It's not a bad thing," he said again. "It has nothing to do with you. I just need to do something else for a while."

"Why?" I asked. There was no answer. There aren't answers to these kinds of questions.

I have, in my life, experienced certain visual disturbances. Occasionally and without warning, the world looks as if it is vibrating very slightly, as if all the molecules and atoms are just raring to explode away from one another. There is also a sense of vertigo, tunnel vision that blurs the edges of my peripheral field, and the combined effect is both distressing and menacing. I no longer need food or sleep when I am in such a state; I am too distracted by the madness and movement. This was how I felt now.

There was nothing to do except pretend normalcy and hope that it would pass quickly, like a cloud in front of the sun. I couldn't bring myself to mind very much. I dressed slowly, applied lipstick, and looked at my bulletproof face in the mirror.

Cal got to the diner a little before closing and sat at the counter. "Where's your guy?" he asked in a loose, conversational tone, as if we had always been friends.

"No clue," I said. It was an approximation of the truth.

Life goes on. I sold the last painting of Red a while back. I graduated from school a semester early and got an internship at the gallery that had exhibited my paintings. My boss was harsh, but fair.

I got a postcard from Red a little while back. All it said was, "How are you?" in his crabbed, crushed handwriting. There was no return address.

"I'm fine, how are you?" I wrote back, but there was nowhere to send it. I hung it on my fridge instead, pinned it down with a magnet shaped like a pea pod. Marmalade, who had since taken up residence in my apartment, wrapped herself around my ankles and meowed plaintively.

"I know," I said to the cat. "I thought so too."

Why Does There Have to Be a Why?

Terry wants to get married. "Why?" I say, lying in bed, mostly naked, smoking one of his cigarettes. "What's the point? We're just going to have to get divorced in a few years anyway."

"You get a tax credit," he says. "And besides, I love you."

"So what?" I say and roll over and go to sleep.

Terry won't let it go though. Terry never lets anything go. It's one of the reasons I keep him around. He's like a bull terrier.

"Aaron," he whines one morning when I'm poaching eggs. "Marry me."

"No," I say. "I don't want to."

"Why not?"

"You know why not," I say. "Besides, why should I?"

"Why does there have to be a why?" Terry lights a cigarette. He's wearing my boxers and one of my good shirts, one from the Salvation Army that I used to wear to teach before they fired me. He sits at my kitchen table like he's at home. I hate that Terry basically lives at my apartment, but he still lives with his ex-girlfriend, and she doesn't know I exist. Don't ever sign five-year leases with a significant other is the moral of that story.

"There's always a why," I say. "Why do you love me?"

"What?" Terry says. "Do you want, like, a list?"

Terry comes to me with a list a few days later. I'm working on the book and not in the mood to be bothered. He sits down next to me at my desk and puts a sheet of paper in front of me.

"What do you want?"

"I made a list," he says and smiles at me. That Terry smile, big and bright. I look at the paper. On it, in his chicken scrawl, are the words:

voice

teeth

pupils

relationship to parents

serious all the time, even during sleep/sex

"What is this?" I say.

"It's the reasons," he says. "Why I love you. Why we should get married."

"These aren't reasons to love someone," I say. I sit back in my chair. "This doesn't make any sense. I don't know what you're trying to do here.

"There were more," Terry says. "These are just the highlights."

"Well, okay," I say. "Leave me alone. I have to work. I have a deadline, if you didn't remember."

"How could I forget?" Terry mock pouts. "Whatever. I'm going to go do laundry."

I turn back to my work, nodding. "You do that."

But when he's gone, I take the list and put it in my shirt pocket.

One night when Terry is somewhere else, I go out to a bar and meet a guy. You know the type. Leather jacket, hair. Smiles. "You wanna get out of here?" he says.

"Oh," I say. "I'm married."

I don't know why I say it. I know Terry fucks other people. I fuck other people. It's not even a thing. But something makes my mouth move, and I can't control it. I feel sick.

"That's okay," the guy says. Smiles again, like a snake. I've had too much to drink.

"I'm going to go to the bathroom," I say.

"Can I come?" he says.

I let him slam my head against the wall and come in my mouth and a hundred other fucked-up things. I don't even care. I just want to think about something other than Terry. God. I think about that list.

voice

teeth

pupils

relationship to parents

serious all the time, even during sleep/sex

Is that all there is? I think about that as I walk home. Someone's voice, someone's teeth. I call Terry. "What?" he says, sounding annoyed.

"Nothing," I say. "I'm not going to marry you."

"I know you're not," he says. "Aaron, I get that."

"Then why do you keep asking me?"

"I don't know," he says. "It's something to fill the time before we die."

"Oh," I say and hang up the phone.

Terry and I get drinks a few nights later. I'm tired and in a bad mood. We make it about fifteen minutes before we start arguing. "What do you mean, you love me?" I say. "What does that mean? We barely know each other. We just fuck and hang out and that's it. Jesus Christ."

"I know you really well," Terry says. "Besides, who says you get to decide who loves who? You're not the king of everything, no matter how much you think you are."

"I don't think that," I say. "I've never thought that."

He grimaces. "Well, you certainly act like this. With your fucking book and your work and all your bullshit."

"I don't have bullshit."

"Oh, yes, you do."

Terry gets up to piss, and I try to calm down. I make a fist with my hands and then take a long drink of my beer.

He comes back, and I see him in the red light of the bar and feel bad. "I'm sorry," I say. "I didn't mean to start a fight with you."

"It's okay," he says. "I forgive you."

"Do you want to go home?"

He nods. "Yeah. Let's go."

I wake up from a nightmare, and Terry is there, his hands in my hair, breathing heavily. His dick is hard against my back. "Shhh," he says. "You had a bad dream."

"I know, I know."

He kisses me, awkward angle, and I try to relax into it but can't. "Stay," I say, even though I know he has to get up for work in a few hours. "Don't go yet."

"Aaron," he says, and I know that in a few minutes he'll be putting on his pants and going home to shower. He puts his hands down my shorts and his hand around my dick, and for a little while, everything goes away. "Aaron," he says again.

"I'm right here," I say. Even though that's not what he wants me to say, it's good enough.

*

I work on the book all morning and smoke the cigarettes Terry left. I start drinking around noon, and by the time Terry gets here, I'm drunk.

"God, you're pathetic," he says and helps me to bed. I have to get up to vomit. "What's wrong?" he asks.

"I don't know," I say, even though I know perfectly well. "I just—"

"Oh, my God," he says, and he looks so smug for a second that I think he's going to walk right out of here. "You don't. You do, don't you?"

"I what?"

"You love me."

"I don't even know why you would say that."

He wipes the vomit from my mouth with a towel. We're sitting on the bathroom floor, the tile cool underneath my bare legs. "It's true," he says. "God, I can't believe it. The mighty Aaron Starr, felled by love."

I think about the list again.

voice

teeth

pupils

relationship to parents

serious all the time, even during sleep/sex

"Shut up," I say and pass out on the bathroom floor. Terry carries me to bed.

*

In the morning I'm hungover and ashamed. Terry is humming, frying eggs. I come into the kitchen. "Fine," I say. "You win. Maybe I do love you, a little bit."

"A lotta bit," he says. "You do, you do."

"Whatever," I say. "I'm still not getting married. To anyone. Ever."

"Uh-huh," he says and puts a plate in front of me.

Why does there have to be a why? Why do we love anyone? I write it in my acknowledgments page. I finish the book.

Some questions don't have answers. And maybe it's better that way.

To Terry. With Love.

Systematic Incompatibilities

Louis has stopped smoking. He doesn't say anything about it, but one morning I find his cigarettes in the trash. I pick them out and smoke them myself, sitting on the deck, before he wakes up. All eighteen of them. I don't know what kind of lunatic would throw out a full pack. If I were going to quit smoking, I would wait until I was in between packs before I quit. I wouldn't buy a new pack and then suddenly stop.

I come back inside reeking of smoke with a pain in my chest. Louis is making coffee. "Good morning," he says.

"If you say so," I tell him. He's used to me though. I'm not a morning person. I take the coffee from him and pour myself a cup. "What do you have going on for today?"

"Work."

"I mean, obviously," I say. "Do you want to tell me about it?"

"Not really."

I remember that he's quitting smoking, so I cut him some slack, walk into the living room, and turn on the TV. The news is depressing. I switch it off. I work from home three days a week. Today I'm supposed to be writing, but I don't feel like it, and already I know it's going to be the kind of day where I don't get anything done. I just have to wait for Louis to leave for work so I can take a Xanax and pass out.

Louis doesn't like me taking pills. We're supposed to be trying to get pregnant, but I'm still taking my birth control pills. Louis does not know this. If Louis knew this, we would have a Problem. Louis hasn't said this, but I know he's quitting smoking because he thinks it'll be better for the baby, or it'll affect our conception, or something. He wants me to quit too, but I tell him I'll quit when I actually get pregnant, which will never happen because I am still on the pill.

We are at an impasse.

I do not want a baby.

I have told Louis this.

"Everyone wants a baby," he says. "You're thirty-five. It's a biological imperative."

My mother also says this. She's on her third marriage, but I'm her only child. "Having a baby changes your life," she says. "You'll see."

"I know it changes your life," I say. "I don't want my life changed. I like my life."

And I do. Or I did. Before Louis and I started trying, life was good. I was a pretty successful freelance hack for a couple of newspapers. I had a book deal, which has now fallen through because publishers are assholes. I got a kill fee though. I got day drunk three days a week at extended brunches and smoked to my heart's content. Louis and I had morning sex. Louis is a chemical engineer, and he's happy at his job. We have a nice apartment in Carroll Gardens. We're living the yuppie Millennial American Dream.

And then our friends started having babies. It started slowly—one or two, here and there. Baby showers. At first I thought it was like the weddings, which started when I was about twenty-five. For a while it seemed like there was a wedding every damn weekend. Louis and I had gotten married just to keep up. But the babies started when I was around thirty, and they didn't stop. Suddenly I was getting plans canceled because "oh no, I can't find a sitter."

No more double dates and friend dinner parties. No more late-night movies.

No more fucking brunch. All anyone wanted to do was walk through Prospect Park on a Saturday afternoon with a Thermos of white wine. I'm going to be very clear here. I don't like children. They're sticky, they're noisy, they're annoying. I've never liked children. I didn't even really like *being* a child. If that makes me a horrible person, well, here I am.

Sue me.

Louis comes into the living room, looks at me in my pajamas, and says, "Are you going to work today?" even though my schedule is color-coded and hung up in the living room.

"Not today," I say. "Working from home."

"Are you at least going to go to the coffee shop or something?"

"I was just going to hang around the house today," I say. "What, is that interrupting your great plans?"

"No," he says and gives me a weird look. Then he walks into the bedroom and I can hear him rifling through his closet.

I go into the bathroom, shake out a Xanax, and swallow it with a glob of spit. I have about thirty minutes before I can't do shit, but I figure Louis will be gone by then. I come out of the bathroom to Louis holding two shirts up in front of me. They're both blue.

"Which one?" he says.

"I don't care," I say.

"Come on, Gina."

I pick randomly. "That one."

"I hate that one."

"Then the other one. Jesus." I go into the bedroom and lie face down on the bed.

We meet at a party when I'm nineteen; he's eighteen. I smoke; he doesn't. Later he picks it up. We joke that I've corrupted him. I call him "Eighteen" as a nickname. We dance in the living room, me in my high heels, shaky ankles. I'm nervous and drunk. Lipstick prints on Modelo cans. Vomiting in the bathroom.

We have sex in his dorm room. Condom wrappers on the floor. Hands where hands go. It's good, as good as it can be. I decide I like him. Tell him I'll text him, someday, maybe. I'm in a slut phase, so maybe I won't. Light a cigarette. Louis. I say his name under my breath, like a mantra. "I'm going to marry that boy," I tell my girlfriends.

"Right," they say. "Sure you are."

He's all limbs and angles, gawky, still got that teenage awkwardness to him. Majoring in chemical engineering. We're in that strange time when you sometimes ask people, "What's your major?" and sometimes ask them, "What do you do?" as if they're the same question. "What do you want to do?" is another one.

I want to be a writer. A journalist, a real one. Hard-hitting stories that change people's lives. Exposés. I want to drink black coffee and shout at someone over the din of the newsroom. I laugh at the poets, the creative writers dressed in all black, smoking their cigarettes outside the lit building. But secretly I write poetry in my notebook, poetry about how Louis looks, naked, in the early light of the morning, and I don't tell anyone, not even him.

the shadow of a ribcage

the smoke in your lungs

I think I love you,

Don't tell

We go on a date. It's a good date, objectively good. He tells me about himself: born in Connecticut, oldest of three siblings, two sisters. He has one tattoo—a knife, on his knee. All the men in his family have the same tattoo; they do it themselves in their own kitchens when they turn eighteen. Lot of military men in his family. They wanted him to join the army, but he was too smart. When he graduated, his father sat him down and said, "Son, I want you to make something of yourself. Be more than a grunt in someone else's army."

So school is important to him. He has to be great. His eyes shine as he tells me this story. I can tell how much his father means to him, how important family is to him. I can picture the house in Connecticut, the smiling mother, the younger sisters. The dog. I want to meet them, I want to charm them. I tell him about me: Rhode Island, sailing summers, only child of artists. An upbringing in an artist's colony. About my desire for a more conventional life, some structure, something to show for myself.

"I want to make something of myself, you know?" I say.

"I agree with that," he says.

And just like that, we are holding hands across the table in this restaurant in Chinatown.

Later we go to a bar. We make out in the back by the bathrooms. "Do you want to go back to my place?" I say. I have an apartment in Brooklyn, three roommates. Twin bed shoved into a corner.

He lays me down on the bed like I'm something precious. Long train ride back to Flatbush, I think. Better stay the night.

My girlfriends all ask what's going on with me. "You're not usually like this," they say. "You don't care about boys. What's going on?"

"I don't know," I say. "He's different."

There are a hundred reasons why people fall in love, and none of them are unique. It's chemical, it's pheromones, it's bullshit. I don't explain any of that to them. Instead, I tell them how he went down on me for an hour when we were drunk and I couldn't finish, but he was determined. I tell them how he held me when I had nightmares. I tell them about the way he sleeps, curled around my body like it's important. I tell them all of these things, and they complain about their boyfriends—doesn't shave, shaves too much, doesn't smoke, smokes too much—and I feel special. Louis and I have not used the B word yet. But it's coming, I can feel it. It lingers in my mouth like a promise.

Louis leaves, slamming the door. The Xanax is making everything watery and hazy. I think about making myself a drink, then remember it's nine in the morning. I settle for smoking another cigarette, then fall asleep on the couch watching reruns. I wake up four hours later with a pounding headache and call my friend Veronica.

"You're doing Xanax again," she says. Veronica has just had her third baby, and she's still on maternity leave from her job as an entertainment lawyer, which is the only reason why she's picking up her phone in the middle of the day. "I can tell by the way you're slurring your words."

"I have to," I say. "My life is a fucking nightmare. Louis won't talk to me. He wants a fucking baby."

"Are you two even having sex?" she says. "You know he'll know something is wrong if you stop having sex."

"We're having sex all the time," I say. "It's the only thing we can do apparently. Morning, evening, night. We don't talk. We just have sex, order Thai food, and have sex while we're waiting for delivery. The other day Louis opened the door with a sock over his dick. I thought the delivery boy was going to start crying."

"And he doesn't know you're still on the pill."

"I can't tell him!" I cry. "He'll lose his mind. He has this idea that if we have a baby, we'll be just like everyone else."

"I hate to break it to you, Gina, but you *are* just like everyone else."

"I know, and I don't care," I say. "I'm happy with the way things are. I don't want a baby ruining everything." I realize what I've just said and who I've said it to, and I feel bad. "I mean, well, you know what I mean."

"I know," she says in that soothing way that she only started using after she had her first kid. "I know, sweetie. Listen. Babies don't ruin things. But they do change things. And if you're going to have one, you have to be prepared for that."

"I don't want things to change," I say, aware that I'm whining. I get up from the couch and pour myself a glass of warm wine. "God, is there something wrong with me? I just don't like babies, okay? I don't think that's so bad."

"It's not bad," she says. "I don't like them either. But here we are."

"You have three," I remind her.

"And God, I cannot wait 'til they go to college and I have my life back," she says. "Jesus, I'll be sixty by the time that happens. Do you think I'll still be hot?"

I smile. "You'll always be hot, V."

We hang up the phone. I feel a little better, but also a little fuzzy. I get my laptop and type out a scathing essay on women over thirty-five and the pressure to procreate, and then delete it because I realize that Louis reads everything I publish, and I could never let him read this. My editor has been haranguing me to write another book proposal, but I can't think of anything worthwhile. My last book, the one that fell through, was a collection of essays about sex and relationships in your twenties. "Too *Sex and the City*," the publishers decided and killed it.

"This is the only thing I know how to do," I tell the cat, who looks up at me with her little face and then retreats to the bedroom.

I'm so alone not even my cat wants to hang out with me. I fall back asleep on the couch.

On our third date, Louis and I go to the movies. The movie is called *You Were Never Really Here,* and it's the story of a brutal enforcer who has to rescue a teenage girl from sex traffickers. It's surreal and violent, and halfway through, Louis says, "Do you want to get out of here?"

I decide right there that this nonviolent boy, this is the person I want to spend the rest of my life with. He can't even kill spiders. He makes me take them outside.

After the movie, we go to a bar in the Village. We sit in the same side of the booth and talk about our classes, about our parents, about our lives and how they are starting to overlap. We kiss and then pretend like we don't want to keep kissing. I want him to meet my friends. He wants me to meet his friends. He gets too excited talking about the periodic table and has to stand up. We go outside, and I smoke a cigarette and he takes drags from it.

I tell him about how I grew up sailing on Rhode Island in the summers, how it feels to have the rope in your fingers and the wind in your hair, the freedom of being out on the water. He tells me he's afraid of boats. I tell him there's something freeing about being out there, in the open water, because there's nothing you can do. If you go down, you go down. Everything is left to fate and how good of a sailor you are. Your life is in your own hands or some god's.

"I don't like that," he says. "I would rather keep my feet on dry land."

Sometimes there are signs. Sometimes you can go back and pinpoint, that was the moment *when.* I don't do this until much later. Much later, though, I do go back, and I see the signs, and I say, "Oh."

When Louis comes home from work, we order Chinese and watch the evening news. I go out for a cigarette four times in two hours. Louis pretends not to be mad about it. I'm drunk, and he knows it, and he doesn't say anything. It used to be he would get drunk with me, but now he won't, and I hate him for it. He's thirty-four and no fun anymore. Around drink number eight, I tell him that to his face.

"Gina," he says. That's all he says.

Then he grabs me by the hair, and we have sex on the living room floor. I get rug burns on my back. After he's finished, he gets up and goes to the bathroom. I lie on my back and feel tired and stupid and drunk. I need to tell him, I think. I need to tell him I don't want a baby.

But when he comes back from the bathroom, all he says is, "I'm going to go to bed."

And then he switches off the TV and goes into the bedroom.

I fall asleep on the floor and wake up there the next morning.

The first time Louis meets my mother, she looks at me, in front of him, and says, "Are you sure?"

"Yes, Ma, I'm sure," I say.

It's Thanksgiving. I've brought him up for dinner, the first winter that we're officially dating. We did about a year of off-and-on, late nights showing up drunk at my apartment, text messages sent and deleted, whatever you do when you're eighteen and in love. Then he says, "Let's make it official."

"What does that mean?" I say.

"Be my girlfriend," he says.

"Okay," I say.

I bring him to Rhode Island that winter. It's a cold one, and we're bundled up in our coats. Louis has put on some weight, and he looks good—I keep telling him how good he looks. He's in his third year of school now; I'm in my fourth. I'm looking at graduate schools, Columbia specifically, and everyone says I'm going somewhere, I'm going to get in, I'm going to make something of myself. Louis has just won a big fellowship, twenty thousand dollars, and we're supposed to be celebrating. I have told my mother about this, but she isn't impressed.

"Chemical engineering?" she says. "What is that, like, science? Is he going to be a doctor?"

"Yeah, Ma, a doctor. A PhD."

"That's a lot of schooling," she says. "Expensive."

"He's got a fellowship," I say. "The school pays for it."

"What?" she says.

She's getting hard of hearing, I think. I have to repeat myself a lot. Sometimes I think she's just faking it because she doesn't want to listen to me. My father has been dead two years, but she hated him. They were never married, but they lived in the same artist's colony for over twenty years. He fucked other women, and she never said anything, but I knew she hated it.

I saw them fight once. "Your daughter shouldn't have to watch you whore around," she said. I didn't hear the rest of the fight.

"Are you sure?" she says, and I know what she's really asking. She's saying, choose wisely because you don't get to choose again. Not really.

"I'm sure, Ma," I say.

"Okay, whatever you say," she says and busies herself in the kitchen.

I wake up fully alert in the middle of the night and know what the new book will be about. It's about women in their thirties who don't want kids. Career women, sure, but also just regular women who like their lives the way they are. Women who don't particularly like kids. Women like me. It doesn't matter that Louis will hate me for it. That's what I need to write about.

I get up and go to my laptop. I dig the deleted essay out of the trash folder and read it back.

It's not about careers or feeling fulfilled, I write. We're allowed to not want kids. If a woman can be as good as a man, then why can't a woman not want kids if a man can?

I bang out an outline, an abstract, and an introduction. By the time I'm finished, it's started to get light out. Louis stirs in bed, sees me at my desk.

"You're writing again," he says.

"I know," I say.

I send a quick email to my editor with the attached pages. She'll be awake in a few hours. Like me, she doesn't sleep very normal hours.

Louis goes back to sleep, or pretends to. I look over what I've written.

It's okay to want things to stay the same, I write. Sometimes that's a good thing.

I close my laptop and get into bed next to Louis. He curves his body around mine, and we fall asleep like that, breathing in tandem.

At our wedding, I find Louis before the ceremony. "Shit," he says. "It's bad luck to see you in your dress, isn't it?"

My dress is white and dumb looking. My mother picked it out. "I don't care," I say. "I needed to see you."

"What's up?" he says. "What's going on?"

He's wearing a tuxedo. All of our friends are out there and my entire extended family.

I look at his face. I love his face. "You look beautiful," he says, as if that helps anything.

"Are you sure you want to do this?" I say. "Like, really sure?"

He laughs. "Of course I'm sure," he says. "I'm sure, I'm sure, I'm sure." He takes my face in his hands. "I knew from the first second I saw you at that party ten years ago. Hell, I started smoking cigarettes because of you. I'll follow you into an early grave."

"You're sure?" I say again.

"Yes," he says. "I'm sure."

"Okay," I say. I'm crying, and my mascara is running. I turn my face up so it doesn't get on my dumb dress. "As long as you're sure."

"Are you sure?" he asks.

"I've never been more sure of anything in my life."

I sleep through Louis leaving for work, which I guess makes sense because I was up all night. I wake up around noon to an email from my editor:

Love these pages. Can't wait to see more.

Then there are some notes, technical stuff, and some ideas about publishers, places we could sell some of the essays to before the whole book comes out. I feel good about this, really good.

I spend the rest of the morning looking through my old notebooks, the ones I kept when Louis and I first started dating. I find a lot of interesting things. Diary entries, stupid teenage musings. I find the poetry I used to write about him before we were married. I want to show him, but I'm also embarrassed. How can you be with someone for so long and not show them something like this?

These days I am trying to be a morning person.
it is hard, like a wound
that will not heal.

I laugh when I find that. I can remember writing it, trying desperately to match myself to Louis's biorhythm. He wakes up early, goes to bed early. I used to love that about him, the way he was productive all the time. Now it just makes me sad because we are so different.

I find this one in another notebook:

You are on my mind,
As always. There is no way
You think about me as often as I think about you.

I want to call Louis at work, but I know he'll be angry if I do. "I love you," I want to say. "Don't you know that?"

I know he does. But sometimes you just want to say it.

Around four I put the notebooks away, get dressed, and go grocery shopping. I cannot remember the last time I left the apartment, and the world seems bright and large and very strange. I buy ingredients for spaghetti bolognese, one of the few things I know how to cook. I text Louis: *Don't order Seamless—I'm cooking tonight.*

He replies: *what?*

I chop ingredients and boil water, and the rhythm of cooking soothes me. For once, I'm not drunk at 6 p.m. For once, my mind isn't foggy in a haze of pills. I'm not wearing sweatpants. I have dinner on the table at 6:30 when he comes home.

"What's going on?" he says. "Oh, my God. You're not—tell me you're not. You're not pregnant, are you?"

"Actually," I say, "it's the opposite."

"What do you mean?" he says, sitting down at the table. "This looks good."

"Well, I guess you could say I have a baby coming," I say. "I talked to my editor this morning, and we're working on a new book project."

"That's great," he says. "Is that what you were working on last night? Baby, I'm so proud of you. I know you were getting into kind of a funk, worried that you weren't going to write anymore."

"I was," I say. "But it's okay now. And you're never going to guess what I found."

"What?" He takes a bite of his pasta, smiles. "This is pretty good, actually."

I ignore the comment. "Some old poetry I wrote when we first started dating. I'll show you. It's pretty hilarious."

He laughs. "I can't wait to see it. So what's this new book about?"

I take a deep breath. "That's what I wanted to talk to you about," I say.

"What's up?"

"The book—" I break off. "It's about women in their thirties who don't want kids."

He is quiet for a moment. "And, what? Are you saying it's, like, based on personal experience?"

"I don't know, Louis. I guess so."

"But we've been trying."

"I know," I say. "I know. But—I haven't stopped taking my birth control pills."

"You what?"

"I haven't stopped taking my birth control."

He stops eating. Stands up. Looks at me. "Give me a cigarette," he says. "I know you still have them. Give me a cigarette, Gina."

I go to the bedroom and get two and hand him one. We go out onto the deck to smoke. He's shaking a little with anger. I can tell he's trying to keep his voice level when he speaks. "Why?" he says.

"I don't want a baby, Louis."

"Why not?"

"I just don't."

"Why not?" he says again.

"I don't like babies," I say. "I never have. I like things the way they are, with just the two of us. I like our life. I love you, and I don't want to change that."

"I think you'd be a great mother, Gina."

"I don't disagree with that," I say. "I just don't want to do it. And I don't want to bring an unwanted child into this world. I think that's fair of me."

He pauses. "Why didn't you tell me this?" he says.

"I didn't know how."

He smokes his cigarette. Thinks. "I don't know, Gina."

"Don't know what?"

"I just don't know," he says.

He drops his cigarette butt off the edge of the deck and lets it fall. "I think I'll sleep on the couch tonight," he says. Then he goes back inside.

I don't sleep. I work on the book, and when I can't write anymore, I lie in bed. I want to go out to the living room, but Louis is out there, and he's awake too. I can hear the deck door opening and closing as he goes out to smoke.

It's four in the morning when the bedroom door opens. Louis comes in, and in the dark, opens his closet, pulls out a suitcase. "I'm sorry, Gina," he says.

"What do you mean, you're sorry?"

"You know what I mean." He puts some clothes in the suitcase. "I think I'm going to go stay with David for a while."

"It's the middle of the night."

"So I'll go to a hotel."

David is his best friend from college. He lives in Prospect Heights. "Don't go," I say. "I'm sorry. I just—I didn't know what to say to you."

"You lied to me."

"I know that."

He looks at me. In the dark, I can barely make out his face, but it doesn't matter because I know it so well. "Gina, I'm really angry about this."

"I know."

"And you don't want a baby. Ever."

"I don't."

"That's that then." He puts some shirts in the suitcase. "I'll come back later in the week to get the rest of my stuff."

"So you're just going to leave?" I pull the covers up to my chest. "That's it? That's the end of it? Sixteen years?"

"I want a baby, Gina."

"I thought you wanted me." I stand up, reach for him. I think about the last time we had sex. On the floor in the living room. I think about our first date. I think about that teenage boy, gawky and awkward, trying to dance to bad music thumping loud in the living room of that apartment. I think about my mother's house on Rhode Island, Thanksgiving dinner. I think about our wedding. I think about standing outside, smoking.

I think about everything. I can't remember the last time he kissed me. He moves away from me.

It's almost five when he leaves. I watch him go. He doesn't say anything else. I don't know what there is for him to say.

We talk on the phone sometimes. There isn't much to say.

"Who wants the coffee table?"

"Do you like that painting in the living room?"

"Can I come by next week and get the rest of my shirts?"

Nights, when I cannot sleep, I work on the book. It is impossible to sleep without Louis. His presence filled the room, even when he wasn't speaking to me. I don't know how to replace it. I write and write, like a dog with a bone. My editor suddenly loves me. *Love this new work ethic,* she writes me in an email. *Keep up the good work.*

I've always been a hard worker, but it turns out that the key to success is the dissolution of a sixteen-year relationship. Who knew?

I start writing blog posts in the middle of the night. I get comments from all over the world, from women like me and not like me, women who say things like:

> My husband wants me to have more children. I tell him no, but I'm worried he's going to sabotage my birth control. What should I do?
>
> I'm thirty-nine, and all I want is to have a baby. Having children is natural. You're a disgrace.
>
> I'm twenty-two, and I just had my third abortion. How do I talk to my mother about it?

To the first, I want to write and tell her to leave him. Take your children and run.

To the second, I want to tell her, best of luck, I'm sorry we have a difference of opinion.

To the third, I have nothing.

I close my laptop and don't reply to any of the comments. My editor told me not to engage with the commenters anyway. It's bad form.

Sometimes there aren't words. I've learned that. Sometimes the best thing to do is to say nothing at all.

In chemistry, there are some substances, like oil and water, that won't mix, no matter how hard you try to mix them. Oil sits on the surface of water, no matter how much you shake the jar. They're systematically incompatible. Louis told me about that once. He likes to use science metaphors for life. He says that the universe is the best metaphor. This is what he tells me when the papers come. This is what he says when I ask him, for the hundredth time, why he is doing this.

"I don't know how to explain this any other way, Gina."

"Stop talking about fucking chemistry right now," I say. I've just been served with divorce papers, and he's come over to talk to me about them. "We were together for sixteen years, and you're just realizing now that we're oil and water?"

"I didn't have to come over at all," he says. "I could have just let you get the papers and have that be that."

"Maybe you should have," I say. It sounds venomous, even to me.

"Look, I'm sorry," he says. "This is the way it is." He puts his hands up.

When he leaves, I throw a glass at the door. It shatters, making a satisfying sound.

I leaf through the papers. It's all legalese, I don't understand a word. *Systematic incompatibilities. Irreconcilable differences.* The words fill my head and keep filling it, and eventually I have to go lie down. I take a Xanax.

On our wedding night, Louis carries me to the bedroom like you see in the movies. "It's not like we haven't done this before," I joke. "Aren't I heavy?"

"Light as a feather," he says and drops me unceremoniously onto the bed. I laugh. He pours me a glass of champagne. I've already had too much, but I drink it anyway. The bubbles go to my head.

"I love you," he says seriously. "I mean it."

"I know you do," I say, which is the wrong thing to say, but also the right thing at the same time.

"And you love me."

"Uh-huh."

He kisses me, and I feel the same way I felt that first night at the party and all of the other times he's kissed me since. My stomach flips, and everything else slides away. Knots unknot themselves in my shoulders. It's another movie moment.

What we do in that bedroom isn't special or unique or important to anyone but us, but to me, it means something. It means that we're in this together, for better or worse.

Louis comes over on Saturday night. We haven't seen each other or spoken for more than five minutes in two months. We're supposed to have dinner, talk about the future. He's gained weight—that's the first thing I notice. He looks okay, not great. "I need to talk to you about something," he says.

I don't like the sound of that and say so. Louis grimaces. I can tell whatever he's about to say isn't going to be easy for either of us. "I've met someone," he says finally. "I've met someone, and she's pregnant."

"Excuse me," I say.

I'm holding a wine glass, and I immediately drop it. It shatters, and Louis goes to get a dustpan. I go out onto the deck. I can't get the cigarette lit. It's January, and I'm not wearing a coat. Louis comes out with the dustpan still in his hands and says, "I'm sorry."

"It's been two months, Louis," I say.

"I know," he says. "I said I was sorry."

"How does 'sorry' even begin to cover it?"

"I'm really sorry," he says.

I get the cigarette lit and smoke it in harsh puffs. "Who is she?"

"Someone from work. Not my department—we met in the breakroom."

"And what, she was just waiting for us to get divorced so she could swoop in?" I can feel myself getting nasty, but I can't help it.

"It wasn't like that."

"Did you fuck her while we were still married?"

"What?" he says. "No. Of course not. Jesus. This is a good thing, okay? We're both getting what we want. We can both move on."

"How am I getting what I want?"

He looks at me. Doesn't say anything. He knows I've got him.

"I wanted to stay with you," I say. "That was the whole point. I wanted to stay married. You were the one who was all, divorce papers, I'm moving out, whatever."

"You lied to me."

"People lie. People get over it." I take a drag of my cigarette, try not to blow smoke in his face "You could have gotten over it."

"I wasn't going to get over it," he says. "I'm still not over it. Gina, she's pregnant. I can't just mosey on back over here and get back with my ex-wife. Even if I wanted to."

"Jesus, haven't you ever heard of the pull-out method?"

"Don't be a bitch."

"How old is she anyway?" I ask. "Twenty-four?"

He pauses. "She's twenty-six."

I throw my hands up. "Great. Perfect. You're shacking up with a twenty-six-year-old, and I'm going to die alone, and the cat is going to eat my dead body."

"You're not alone," he says. "You have tons of friends. And you have the book."

"My friends all have babies," I point out. "And the book isn't going to keep me warm at night."

"I don't know what you want me to do," Louis says. "This is what's happening."

"I'm just, I don't know, expressing my annoyance." I crush my cigarette out and toss it off the edge of the deck. "You're officially uninvited from dinner by the way."

"I figured."

"Good." I go back inside. Louis has cleaned up the broken glass, but now we only have five wine glasses. I walk him to the door. "Congratulations," I say. "I know this is what you wanted."

He looks at me in a funny way. "I wanted a baby with you," he says finally. "That's what I really wanted."

Then he leaves, leaving me to feel like a piece of shit.

*

People tell me I'm better off when they hear. People tell me I'm being brave. I don't feel better off. I don't feel brave. I feel tired most days, and it doesn't feel like I can ever get enough sleep. Oil and water. Systematic incompatibilities. Two puzzle pieces that look like they're going to go together, but when you line them up, you realize they don't fit at all.

This is what I think about at night. When I can't sleep. Veronica tells me to take an Ambien, but for once I don't think pharmaceuticals are the answer to all my problems. I lie awake and stare at the ceiling. The cat sleeps on my legs. It's a strange thing, being alone. I didn't think about it that much when I was married, the fact that I was rarely by myself. I worked alone, I guess, but when I was home, there was always someone there, even if we weren't talking. Louis sitting on the couch. Louis making himself a piece of toast. Louis, Louis, Louis.

I feel the need to start over. I want to start from the beginning, but that's not possible. There's no reverse button, no way to go back and change things that have already been done. I know that at some point I'll have to begin the massive project of getting to know someone again, learning their likes and dislikes and when they like to have sex and what their favorite foods are, their schedules and rhythms, but I'm not there, not yet. I know I might have this same fight again. I'm thirty-five—not old, but not a child either. People fall in love all the time—it's not difficult. But at the same time, how many do we get? You have to wonder. Maybe it's more than you think. Maybe it's less.

Unsaid Things

They didn't talk about it, not at first. Later they would talk for hours, and none of it would make any difference. Annie tried to tell him, "This is my understanding of pain. It's different than yours. But it's mine."

He didn't understand what she meant. For Walter, pain was something that happened to you, something you experienced. He didn't see it as something that could be interpreted differently. For him, pain was pain, just like water was wet, and when he went out in the rain, he assumed his wet hair felt the same against his neck as everyone else's. Annie didn't ask, "what if you got a buzz cut?" because he would have laughed and asked, "why would I ever get a buzz cut?"

She tried to talk to him about pain tolerance, about how women handled pain better than men, about pain psychology and threshold. He had no patience for science. He assumed that because they had both suffered a loss, they would be kindred spirits. But he had lost a girlfriend, and she had lost a sister. Their losses were not interchangeable, even as Annie wished they were.

He was the one person who Annie thought would understand her. But she had a lifetime of memories of her sister, and he had only a few short months at university and then several years of longing afterward. He had never really gotten over her. Annie had known that, but hadn't picked up the phone when he had called, all those years ago, trying to reach her. Everyone was always trying to reach her sister, she thought. Clara.

Walter and Clara's courtship was brief and intense. Annie remembered Clara calling her late in the night, Clara's first year at college in Georgia. Annie was in New York, smoking cigarettes in the rain, and almost didn't pick up the phone. She was with a man, one of a series of men who she would find ultimately unsatisfying. They were Irish twins, Clara thirteen months older. Annie had come to New York to be an artist, but she wasn't enrolled in school and spent her days lazing around Bushwick, hanging out in coffee shops, waiting for something to happen to her. Clara was pre-med at Georgia Tech, making their parents proud with her A grades in chemistry. She called Annie, and it was raining, but Annie picked up the phone.

"I met someone," Clara said breathlessly into the phone. "Annie, I met someone."

"Okay," Annie said. The man she was with was standing next to her. She could feel him listening to the conversation. She turned to him. "Sorry, it's my sister."

"I met him at a party," Clara was telling her. "His name is Walter."

"Walter isn't a sexy name," Annie said.

"He's very sexy," Clara said.

"Look, I'm outside, and it's raining," Annie said. "I'll talk to you tomorrow." She hung up the phone on her sister. In the morning, they would talk, she told herself. When the skies had cleared up some. Then she didn't give it another thought, turning to the man who was waiting for her.

It wasn't as if Clara was always meeting guys. Clara was pretty, but she wasn't so pretty that people stopped on the street to stare at her. And there was something about her, something awkward, something fragile, that made it difficult to approach her. Annie was always the popular one, even though she was younger. Clara was protective of Annie, but Annie knew Clara was envious of the attention Annie got. When they were teenagers, Clara seventeen and Annie sixteen, they got into screaming matches about who was taking whom to prom and homecoming.

"You always try to take everything away from me," Clara said, a reprisal of the same fight they had been having since they were children. A Barbie doll, their mother's attention, a piece of dessert. Annie always wanted whatever was on Clara's plate.

"I don't want my own," Annie would pout, stomping her small foot on the floor. Their mother would be offering her something, something to calm her down. "I want some of yours."

So it wasn't as if she had a lot of boyfriends. Clara was the studious one; Annie was the rebel. Clara got good grades, made their parents proud, while Annie made them hang their heads in shame. When Annie was seventeen, she caught her mother trying to cut up her expensive leather pants with scissors. Clara was the golden child, and Annie resented her for that, although she never would have put that emotion into words.

Annie's boyfriends came and went like the wind. She was too wrapped up in her own shambles of a love life to pay much attention to her sister's. Still, when Walter made an appearance at Thanksgiving dinner that fall, she took notice. It was impossible not to notice him. He was sexy. He had that easy charm that made girls like her sister fall in love. Annie thought he was sleazy. He was a football player. He had shoulder-length golden hair and green eyes like chips of green ice. He joked with their father, complimented their mother on her cooking. After dinner, he went outside with Annie to smoke a joint.

Annie had heard all about him from her sister, over phone calls and emails, text messages when he had done something particularly cute, and it felt good to put a face to the name. It was hard not to like Walter, although she tried her hardest. They passed the joint back and forth.

"What's your intention with my sister?" Annie said.

"She's a great girl," Walter said. "You know, I think I might love her."

Annie wasn't sure she believed in love as a concept at all. "Sure you do," she said. "My sister puts out."

She knew all about their sex life through Clara's stories. Annie had long shocked Clara with tales of her own exploits, and finally Clara had something to reciprocate.

"It's not about that," Walter said, exhaling smoke. "I really do care about her."

"I've heard that before," Annie lied. She hadn't. Not about Clara. "Well, listen. As her sister, you have to know that if you hurt her, I'll take a shovel to your balls.

He chuckled, a low, dirty sound. "Right."

"I mean it," Annie said. "I have no remorse."

"I'm sure you don't," he said.

Annie assumed that Clara had told him all about her, just like Clara had told Annie all about Walter. The weed was making her feel fuzzy, and suddenly the whole thing just seemed absurd. Her sister, with the sleazy, weed-smoking football player. Her, threatening to hurt him. It seemed so obvious that it wouldn't last, and it didn't. In three months, he had cheated on her, and Clara was throwing him out of her apartment.

Annie thought that was the last she would hear from Walter. She was deeply involved, by that time, with a married man she had met at a bar by her apartment. So when an unlisted number called her phone, she assumed it was her married lover and was extremely surprised to hear Walter's sloshy voice on the other end. He was drunk.

"How did you get this number?" she asked. "Hello? Walter? Why are you calling me?"

"You have to talk to your sister about me?" he said, panting into the receiver. "You have to tell her that I'm sorry. That I love her. That the other guys were with me and I just didn't know how to say no."

"What?" Annie said. She hadn't really been paying attention when her sister told her about Walter's cheating, which had involved a strip club, some football players from the Georgia Tech team, a hooker, and her sister accusing Walter of exposing her to diseases. It was a fairly interesting story, sure, but Annie was too self-involved to care. Besides, the connection was bad. "Walter, you're breaking up."

"I know we broke up," he said, not understanding what she meant. "But I love her. You have to tell her that I'm sorry, I love her, I'm sorry." And then he started crying, crying into the phone.

"Walter, I'm not going to tell her anything," Annie said. "She's your girlfriend. You deal with it."

It wasn't the last time he would call. Over the years, Annie came to expect the calls when she least expected them. Whenever she would relax, even a little bit, she would get a call from an unknown number and find Walter on the other end, crying, begging her to talk to Clara. Soon he just started asking for news of her, if she was dating anyone new, if she ever talked about him. Annie assured him that she didn't. Finally Annie just stopped picking up the phone. She never told Clara about these phone calls. She figured Clara wouldn't care, and besides, she didn't want to hurt her sister any more than she had already been hurt. Her sister had always been fragile.

Life went on. Annie broke up with the married man, started dating the man who would later be her husband. Clara was dating some, mostly nice guys from her pre-med program, and then she got into medical school and was on her way to becoming a doctor. Annie got a job working as a graphic designer at a firm in the city. She got married. She was expecting her first child, and Clara was in her third year of residency when she got the call.

The call was short and to the point. Her mother's voice on the other end. "Your sister is dead," her mother said.

"What?" Annie said.

"The funeral is next weekend," her mother said. "Please, come home."

Annie found out from the newspaper that Clara had killed herself. Her parents wouldn't speak of it. Annie called Clara's roommate in Atlanta, who had found her. Her sister had come home from a twelve-hour shift at the hospital, drunk a fifth of vodka, taken her entire prescription for Klonopin, and then hung herself from the shower rod. She hadn't been taking any chances.

"It was as if she had to be really, really sure it was going to work," Clara's roommate said. "They always say suicide is a cry for help, but I think she just wanted to die."

Annie didn't have to ask why she did it. There was no why. She wasn't meant for this world. She was a giver, she gave and gave, and never asked for anything. No matter how much she would complain that Annie was taking her things, she always let Annie take them. Annie knew what happened. She gave and gave until it was too much and she had nothing left. She had no more purpose in the world. So she left it.

Annie tried to feel sad about it, but in some ways, she felt sorry for her sister. Clara always had such a hard time. She had tried so hard. In some ways, it was easier. Besides, it meant Annie didn't have to worry about her anymore.

*

Annie wasn't surprised to see Walter at the funeral. She wasn't sure how he knew Clara was dead because they weren't on speaking terms. He hadn't called Annie in about six months. For all she knew, *he* was dead. But there he was, in an ill-fitting black suit, standing by the casket, tears in his eyes. It seemed right. He was, Annie realized, the great love of Clara's short life. It was right that he was there.

"It's good to see you," Annie said to him at the wake. He smelled strongly of vodka and aftershave. He had a beer belly, and his football muscle had all slid into fat. "You look good."

It was a lie, but it was a kind lie, the kind of you tell at weddings and funerals. His glorious blond hair was tangled around his shoulders. He still kept it long, like how he had in college. Annie knew from his phone calls that he had a midlevel job at a business firm in Connecticut. He was married, like Annie was. Two little girls.

Annie's husband hadn't come down for the funeral. "You don't have to," she had told him. "It'll just be depressing for you."

"If you say so, honey," her husband had said. He was very agreeable. It was one of the reasons she had married him.

Walter was married, but clearly he had never gotten over Clara. He cried openly during the funeral ceremony, and now he looked like he was barely holding it together. He had a beer in his hand, which was shaking imperceptibly.

"It's good to see you too, Annie," he said. "You don't still smoke cigarettes, by any chance?"

"Actually," Annie said, "I'm pregnant."

"That why you're not drinking either?" he said. "I quit smoking two years ago, but if there were ever a cause for a smoke, this is it. Maybe I can bum one off your younger cousins."

He didn't say "congratulations." Annie guessed he was so wrapped up in his own grief he couldn't be happy for someone else. "Say," he said. Annie was struck by the word. "You wouldn't want to get out of here, would you? I know you can't drink, but you can certainly watch me drink."

Annie thought about it. Part of her wanted to stay, be with her parents. But he was right. This was a depressing affair, and she wanted out of it as much as he did. "You can be my designated driver," Walter said.

And with that, he took Annie's hand, and they walked out of the wake. They got into his car. Annie drove his big, clunky suburban SVU down slick streets. It was raining, and Annie remembered that it had been raining when she had first heard Walter's name. It seemed right that it was raining, somehow clean. Everything was coming full circle.

Walter made Annie stop at a gas station so he could buy cigarettes. He didn't seem to care that she was pregnant. He blew smoke out of the passenger-side window and said nothing. They drove and drove and finally got to the bar. Annie knew the bar already. They were in her hometown, rural Georgia, and there was only one bar. Annie didn't need to use the GPS to know how to get there; she just knew.

She didn't ask Walter if he had ever been there before. He affected a strange familiarity when he sat down, but maybe that was just how he felt in bars. She could imagine him sitting in bars alone in his hometown, ordering a whiskey, neat. She realized she didn't know where he was from. She didn't know very much about him at all. She had never listened when Clara had talked about him and never listened when he talked about himself. Now she wished she had.

Walter ordered a whiskey soda. He sipped it slowly. Annie didn't know why, but she had expected him to drink quickly. He had a kind of desperation about him. The bartender was an older woman who called everyone "hon." There was almost no one else in the bar. It was afternoon on a Saturday. Annie asked for a Sprite. The bartender gave her a funny look but brought it anyway with a sad smile. Annie kept waiting for Walter to say something, but he didn't. Finally Annie did.

"You know she killed herself, right?"

She wasn't sure if he knew. She said it casually, as if bringing up the weather.

"I know," he said. "Of course she did."

"She wasn't right for the world," Annie said. She had been harboring this thought for days, mulling it over. She had recalled a memory of her sister as a child, crying when she found a dead bird on the lawn. It had gotten confused and flown into the side of the house. Clara had cradled the bird in her hands and insisted they bury it in the backyard. It was then that Annie knew Clara would go to medical school. Annie didn't know how she knew that Clara would never really become a doctor, but she knew, somehow, that she wouldn't make it that far. "She was too good."

"It's easy to say that the dead are good," Walter said.

"She was good," Annie said, stunned. "You know she was. You loved her."

"I loved her," he said, relishing the past tense. "I loved her." He paused. "But she wasn't all good. She had her difficulties, just like everyone else."

He asked Annie if she remembered Clara's depressions. Annie did, sort of. She remembered moments when Clara had seemed depressed. But that was Clara; mercurial, temperamental. She always had been.

"They would come and go," Walter said. "Every couple of months, she just wouldn't be able to get out of bed." He paused, sipped his drink. "I caught her trying to slit her wrists once."

"What?"

"She made a couple of scratches and then gave up. I found her in the bathtub, crying, bleeding. I don't think she was really trying to hurt herself."

"And you didn't tell me? Our parents?"

"I was just a kid," Walter said. "Fuck. I was nineteen years old. I didn't know what to do. Other than watch her all the time. Jesus, I spent every waking minute with that girl, trying to make sure she wasn't going to do it again."

"Until you couldn't anymore," Annie said.

"You really know how to make a guy feel like shit," he said. "I feel bad for your husband." He grimaced and then realized what he had said. "Sorry." He looked away, ordered another drink. They sat in silence until it came, and he drank deeply. Annie stared past him, at the paintings on the wall. They were all sad velvet paintings. "Yeah, I couldn't deal with it. It was too much. She was too much. I figured she'd be better off without me."

"You're a coward," Annie said. She didn't know why she said it. She just did.

"Hey," he said. "You knew she was unhappy. And you didn't do anything either."

"You're drunk," Annie said. She felt like she should be defending herself. Possibly he had already been drunk at the wake, or possibly the whiskeys had hit him too hard.

"I'm not," he said, although he was. "Face it. She's dead, and it's your fault as much as it's mine."

Annie realized what was happening all at once. He wanted to wallow in his grief. He thought his grief was the same as hers. He wanted to be sad, and he wanted someone to be sad with. But Annie wasn't sad. She felt relieved. Her sister was dead, and she felt relieved. Clara didn't have to suffer anymore.

"It wasn't anyone's fault," Annie said.

"I'm not a good person," Annie said.

Annie didn't mean to sleep with him. But she did. Stumbling out of the bar, his hands on her waist, she asked him where he wanted to go. He had a hotel room, he told her.

"I'll get you home," she said. She did not say, "I'll go home with you." She did not say, "Let's go together." It was something that happened, like falling down a flight of stairs. She lay at the bottom and stared up at the stairs, confused at how her own legs and feet had failed her so gravely.

They drove in silence. Rain beat down on the car roof. His hand drifted down to clamp down on her thigh. That was when she knew. He still had some of the old glamour about him, the tangle of golden hair, the cigarette smoke. She let him put his hand on her thigh, and then they were in his hotel room, and they drank in each other's grief until there was nothing left between them anymore.

They fell upon the bed, clutching each other, fingers crawling into the seams of each other's clothes. Annie didn't think of her husband, of the baby. She thought only of Clara, of how she must have felt, crushed under Walter's body in some dormitory room bed looking over his shoulder to see if her roommate was coming back anytime soon. Now she was feeling that feeling. She thought of what Clara would say if she knew: "You always want what's mine."

And Annie did; it was true. Everything Clara had, Annie wanted. It was pathological. Now Clara was dead, and Annie wanted to be dead too.

"You left me," Annie wanted to say.

"I can't do this without you," Annie wanted to say.

Annie had lived an entire life in the shadow of her sister, and now her sister was gone and she was in the sun. She never thought her sister was protecting her, trying things out so she wouldn't fall on her face when she inevitably got there. Now it seemed that was the only thing Clara had ever done.

"You look like her," Walter said, tracing the bones in Annie's back.

"Don't say that," Annie said. "Don't compare me to her."

Annie had spent her whole life trying to get away from her sister. She never thought that maybe, Clara had been trying to get away from her too.

*

Later, after whatever passion between them had dissipated, they talked about her. Clara. Walter thought Annie would understand how he was feeling. She did and she didn't. He had tried to get away from her, just as Annie had, because he couldn't handle her. She felt the same. Clara had always been too much—emotions too strong, whims too powerful. She was the smart one, sure, but she had also been deeply troubled. Annie could see that in the immediacy of her phone calls, in the long silences between them. Walter had seen it too. He couldn't deal with it. But he had loved her, just as Annie had.

"You don't understand," Annie said. "We were so close in age, we were connected. We were like twins. I knew all of her thoughts before she had them, and she knew mine."

"Did you know when she died?" Walter rolled over onto his back, pulling the covers off of Annie's legs and onto his own. "Like, could you feel it?"

Annie thought about it. "No," she said. "I tried for a long time to stifle that part of me. The part of me that was her. I guess it finally worked."

When she died, around 6 a.m., Annie had been asleep. She hadn't had any dreams that night, hadn't had any feeling that something was wrong. But she hadn't felt any surprise when she heard either.

"She was the only woman I've ever really loved," Walter said.

Annie knew, then, that she had made a mistake. She had known that already, but now she was sure. She had reached out for comfort to the only person she had thought would understand how she was feeling, but he didn't understand at all.

"You didn't even know her," she said, standing up. He was experiencing Clara's death as a loss. Annie was experiencing it as a beginning. "You knew her almost ten years ago."

"But I loved her," he said. "Love doesn't just wear off because you get older."

"Maybe not," Annie said. "But maybe it does."

Annie got on a plane to New York the next morning. She thought about Walter the whole time. He was sad and she was sad, but their sadness was different. Hers was deeper, darker, and it was a sadness for the loss of her sister, but it was also a sadness for the loss of a part of herself. In a way, she felt better knowing Clara was dead. In a way, Annie was happy.

Walter was dumb with grief. Maybe he would never recover. Maybe he would. She wasn't sure. She looked at him when she left, sleeping in the hotel bed, and felt pity for him.

"This is my understanding of pain," she told him before she left. "You have yours."

Annie knew Clara would have been angry that she had slept with Walter. Maybe that was why she had done it. To get back at her for leaving. To take what was hers, which she had been doing her whole life. Now that Clara was gone, how would Annie know what she wanted? Now that she was gone, who would Annie try to be like?

Annie took an early morning flight and arrived in New York as the sun was rising. It was a new day. Her sister was dead. She was alone in the world.

She looked at the sunrise, which her sister would never see. Her husband was picking her up from the airport. She didn't know what she would tell him. Maybe he didn't need to know.

Sometimes we just do things. Sometimes we don't know why.

"I don't want my own," she told Clara over her shoulder. "I want some of yours."

How Does One Feel Close to Another Person?

"How does one feel close to another person?"

I ask Fargo this question on a Thursday night after we're done having sex. He looks at me, like, Caroline, come on. He hates when I do this, run surveys at him. I also do this to my class. I'm teaching history this semester, history and politics, and my students are tired of me, even though it's only halfway through the semester. Too bad, I tell them. I haven't even done midterm grades yet. We've barely even scratched the Industrial Revolution.

Fargo and I have been together four years. In that time, we've had two pregnancy scares, one abortion, gotten engaged, broken up, gotten back together, gotten a dog, gotten rid of said dog, and moved in together. He's always saying, "Caroline, you know this isn't the end of the line," but he never seems to leave for good, and I never seem to find anyone better. I'm thirty-two, which means that, according to the odds, I probably won't. I want kids, and he wants kids, but neither of us really wants kids with each other. Or right now.

After the last pregnancy scare, Fargo looked at me hard and said, "Caroline, we need to talk." I said, "Okay." He said, "I don't want this to be where I end up in ten years, you know what I mean?" I told him he could move his stuff out by the end of the week. But he didn't, and I didn't, and a year later we're still here. I don't know when he's moving out. I call him my boyfriend when my mom calls to ask how I'm doing or when my girlfriends and I get together for book club. But I don't ever ask him if that's the right word. I think I'm afraid of the answer. I don't know what he tells his friends.

"I'm being serious," I tell him Thursday night. "How does one feel close to another person? I think I'm bad at it."

"I know you're bad at it," he says. "You're really bad at it. That's part of the reason we could never work out."

I used to like that Fargo was straightforward, but now it just hurts. "You aren't going anywhere," I say, lightly tapping his shoulder. We're naked, and he's holding me. "Do you feel close to me right now?"

"I did, about thirty seconds before you asked that question," he says. "Now I'm not so sure."

"Oh," I say. "Right."

"Caroline," he says. I used to love the way he said my name. "Go to sleep, okay?"

"I'm trying," I say, even though my mind is alert. I know I won't sleep for hours. I start planning tomorrow's lesson plan in my head to calm myself down.

"I can hear you plotting," he says, stroking my hair. "Stop plotting."

"I'm not plotting. I'm planning," I say. I put my hand on his chest. His thigh rests on my thigh. "Shut up. I'm trying to think."

"You're the one who started talking to me."

"Do you want to have sex again?" I ask.

"I'm tired," he says. But I know he does. Fargo says if you don't do it twice, it doesn't count.

Friday morning I ask my class, "How do you feel close to another person?"

"Intimacy," someone says.

"What does this have to do with the Industrial Revolution?" someone says.

I shoot that student a look. "There's always a method to my madness, you know that," I say. They're used to me by now. "Come on, more answers." I start every class like this, with a question. Sometimes it's a simple yes-or-no; sometimes it's more complicated. The question always has something to do with the lecture, however tenuous the connection, but it also always has some connection to my life. They don't know that part though. I use this class as a testing ground for my own bizarre ideas.

"Sex," a joker in the back shouts out.

"Good," I say, writing it on the board. I love using the board—it gets covered in my insane scribbles every single class.

"Talking to people," someone else says.

We get a pretty good list going.

Intimacy. Sex. Talking to people. Sharing things. Eye contact.

The list goes on. Then I start my lecture. Factories, child labor laws. It's boring stuff, but the students are here to learn. It's an undergraduate lecture course, not the most fun, but I have ways to make it interesting. When I got my PhD, I spent a year studying under my mentor, Dr. Stevens. "Call me Stevie," he said. I never learned more about teaching than I did working as his TA that year. He had this way of making students think they were having ideas, but they were really his ideas regurgitated to him. He coaxed and cajoled until even the shyest students were shouting their ideas from the back of the classroom. I've never seen anything like it.

I'm not him. But I have a few tricks up my sleeve.

"The Industrial Revolution," I finish, "was about machines taking over the roles of people. Can anyone think of a similar revolution in our own times?"

"When smartphones took over the world," someone says.

"And what was the biggest worry then?"

"That people wouldn't be able to connect with each other anymore." I love asking leading questions, questions with obvious answers, so the students feel like they're participating, even when the answer is right in front of their face.

"Whenever machines start doing something that people used to do, we worry that people will become obsolete," I say. "But being close to a person will always be the most important thing you can do. Remember that. Why do we get close to other people?" I write this question on the board. "Exit survey. Why do we get close to other people?"

"Because it feels good," someone says. I don't even look to see who said it. I write it on the board.

"That's it," I say. "Class dismissed."

After class, I see I have two missed calls from Fargo. I call him back. "What's up?"

"I got goddamn fired," he says.

Fargo is a corporate acquisitions lawyer. "What?" I say.

"Well, not fired," he says. "Put on indefinite leave."

"What happened?"

"I—I took a swing at one of the partners."

"What?"

"He was saying some really stupid shit, something about one of our clients, and I don't know, it just happened. We were drunk."

"Are you drunk right now?" I check my watch. It's barely 2 p.m. "Jesus, Fargo."

"We won our case this morning. We all went out to celebrate, and he was running his mouth, and I just lost my temper. I'm sorry. I'll figure it out. We're going to have a meeting on Monday to talk about next steps, but probably. Shit. Probably I'm fucked."

"I don't know what to tell you, Fargo," I say. "You shouldn't have done that."

"I know that, Caroline, Jesus. Do you think I don't know that?"

"I'm sorry, okay, I'm sorry."

I can hear him exhaling deeply. "Go home," I say. "Sleep this off. You'll figure it out. Maybe he'll sleep it off too, and you'll figure it out in the morning."

"You're right," he says. "I didn't actually hit him. Maybe it'll blow over. What are you doing right now? I really need to see you."

"Fargo," I say. "I'm supposed to have a meeting later, with my mentor, to talk about my book. And I have office hours. I'll be home tonight, probably late. It's going to be okay."

"Okay," he says. There's a beat where he would usually say, "I love you." But we haven't said that to each other in a long time. Not since—I don't even know when.

"Okay. See you soon."

My student Kenneth is early to my office and is already standing at the door when I get there. I have a coffee and bagel in hand, lunch, and I feel flustered, even though I'm technically not late. Kenneth is twenty-one and still has that bright-eyed, bushy-tailed undergraduate look about him. His papers are sharp and incisive, full of grammatical errors, and I've been trying to beat the sloppiness out of him. "You could be such a smart academic," I say, "if you just learned to proofread."

Kenneth wants to talk about his paper on the Industrial Revolution, but I'm finding it hard to focus. Instead, we talk about his impending graduation at the end of the term and what his plans are for the future, while I finish my bagel and sip my coffee. I've written him a letter of recommendation for graduate school, and now we're just waiting to hear back from the schools he's applied to: NYU, Columbia, CUNY

Graduate Center. It's March, which means he should be hearing soon. I remember when I applied to graduate school, that combination of fear and elation that comes with applying, the feeling of the future spooling out in front of me like a red carpet.

Now the future seems strangely limited. Whatever I'm doing with Fargo is one thing. A baby, probably soon. Sooner rather than later. And my academic career, which has been stagnant, for the most part. I've been in adjunct hell for almost ten years with no full-time position in sight. I've published a fair amount, but those jobs just don't exist anymore. My mentor says I need a big-name paper, a book deal, but I don't have a research topic that I'm interested enough in or funding to do a big project.

"Professor?" Kenneth says, shaking me out of my thoughts. "Are you all right?"

"What?" I say. "Sorry. I'm just thinking. And, Jesus, call me Caroline. For the last time."

"Well, you are my professor." Kenneth smiles sheepishly. He looks all of twenty-one, all limbs and shaggy blond hair.

"Sorry, it's just been a long day."

"Everything okay?"

"Yeah, I just—my boyfriend, he lost his job today. I should really be at home with him. But I have this meeting later with my mentor to discuss my next project. And I have all this research to do for my next book, which is on the history of the noir novel in the 1950s. I've told you about that, right?"

"Right," he says. I can see his eyes start to glaze over. "Intersection of history and fiction?"

"Right. Using all my fancy degrees. I was a writer in another life, I think."

"In another life." He smiles at me, earnest and strange. "Is your boyfriend going to be okay?"

"Of course. Fargo always lands on his feet. Anyway—you wanted to talk about your paper?"

"Yeah. I thought—did you read it over? The transitions are getting to me again. I don't know how to move from the introduction to the next section."

We talk about transitional phrases for a little while, and it feels good, it feels good to be normal. Everything is going to be fine, I tell myself. But at the same time, I can't help worry about Fargo and wonder what I'm going to come home to tonight. Is he going to be blackout drunk and mean? Passed out on the couch? Crying? There are too many possibilities.

We exist in multiplicities. My mentor always says that. I exhale. He'll make me feel better. Seeing my mentor always grounds me.

When Fargo and I had our first pregnancy scare, I was twenty-nine, and we had only been dating six months. "Hey, why not?" he said when I told him I was late. "We like kids. You have a good job, I have a good job. Let's just do it."

"We're not married," I said.

"Do you want to get married?" he said.

"No," I said. "I mean, I don't know. I'm only twenty-nine. When do people get married?"

I realized later that the answer was, I didn't want to get married to Fargo. There was nothing wrong with Fargo, not at all. He was a nice guy with a good job. But he was boring. He spent a lot of his time watching Sports Center. He didn't like going out to eat or to the movies. He didn't like dogs or cats, so a pet was out of the question. I had no doubt that he would be a good father—he was great with my nieces and nephews when I invited him to Thanksgiving dinner the first winter that we were together. My mother elbowed me and said: "This one, this one's a keeper."

But I just couldn't see myself ending up with a guy like Fargo. All through college and graduate school, I had dated artsy types, musicians who had written songs about me, losers who had stood me up and stolen my credit cards and generally treated me like shit. But they had at least been interesting. Fargo's idea of a fun night out was to watch a movie on Netflix, have sex, and be in bed by 11 p.m. It was nice to be around him, sure, but was this how I was going to spend the rest of my life?

So when the pregnancy test came back negative, I was relieved. I had a reason to break up with him. Instead, though, I found myself relaxing into his arms for what was supposed to be breakup sex but turned into me staying the night. Four years later, we don't like each other much, but I'm still around. What is it about him? We're codependent, sure. But all couples are codependent to some extent. I can't put my finger on it.

I need Fargo. But why do I need him?

The bar where I meet Steve isn't one I'm familiar with. It's on Franklin Avenue, a little out of my way, but I don't mind coming out here. My mentor, Steve, lives in Crown Heights with his wife and two kids. Teaches at Columbia. I've known him since graduate school, which now seems like eons ago. I get there ten minutes early and order a beer, a Tecate. It comes with a lime. I'm halfway through it when he shows up. He's in his fifties but looks forty-five, smells like cigarette smoke, and takes a seat facing the door. We haven't seen each other in almost nine months.

"I have so much to tell you," I start.

"I'm sure you do," he says. "You've been emailing me a lot."

"It's been a crazy semester," I say. "Fargo and I, we, we've been talking about babies, and that's just been a whole cloud hanging over my head because there's never a good time, you know? And I have this book deal, which is a nightmare. I'm so behind on research, and I don't even know if it's interesting enough to make into a book, and I'm terrified of failure. I'm chewing my fingernails to the quick. My students hate me, except for one. He's the best one. I think I'm going to get fired. Do you want to do a tequila shot?"

Steve laughs. He's used to me and my escalating mania. He orders a glass of wine and no tequila shot. "Your birthday is coming up, isn't it?" he says.

"Thirty-three," I say.

"God," he says. "When I met you, you were, what? Twenty-two? Was that really ten years ago?"

"I think it was," I say. "Can you believe that? I was just a baby."

"And now you're going to have a baby."

"I don't know," I say. "We want to. But we don't want to have a baby with each other. We don't really like each other anymore, you know? I think it's over. I think it's just a force of habit."

"I've been married," Steve says. "I get it."

I laugh. "Your marriage isn't like that."

He doesn't say anything for a moment. I listen to the silence. Then I tell him: "Fargo got fired today."

"What is he going to do?"

"I don't know. He needs support, and I don't want to give it to him. We'll just end up tied to each other for even longer. We should just make a clean break now, before we end up married and stuck together forever."

"Do you want to go out for a cigarette?" Steve asks.

"Steve," I say, "I don't smoke anymore."

"Well, come stand outside with me while I smoke."

I get up, taking my beer outside with me. We go to the backyard, and he lights his hand-rolled cigarette. The smell reminds me of being in college.

"What do I do?" I ask him.

"I can't answer that question for you."

"How does one feel close to another person?"

"What?"

"Let's just quit our jobs and move to a cave somewhere and write and not talk to anyone and never look back."

He looks at me, a funny expression on his face. "You know what would happen if we did that, right?"

A chill runs down my spine. I look at him. He's got a look on his face, a look I've never seen before. Like I'm an object and not a person. Like I'm a thing. "Stevie," I say. "I didn't mean it like *that*."

He grimaces. "I'm just saying, that's what would happen. If we ran away together."

"I don't think so. I respect you too much. I've looked up to you since—I don't know when. Since I was twenty-two."

"And I respect you," he says. "And I want us to stay friends. Look, now I've upset you." He makes another sour face. "You won't even look at me."

He tosses his cigarette butt on the ground. He looks like he doesn't know what to say. He looks upset. But then he smiles at me, a sheepish smile. Like a little boy who has been caught doing something wrong.

"I would never forgive you," I say quietly.

"We would never forgive each other," he says decisively.

"That's not what I said," I say. I want him to know that what he said is not okay.

He's silent a moment. "Let's go back inside," he says.

By the time I get home, I'm drunk. Steve and I drink for another four hours. We rehash the past, talk about old colleagues and old friends, old research papers. We talk about the future, about his tenure at Columbia, about his forthcoming book and mine. We talk about his wife, about his kids, about my potential for childbearing. We don't talk about the awkward moment outside, and something tells me it will never come up again. But something about it unnerves me. I never knew that he thought of me like that, that he was even capable of thinking of me like that, and the knowledge hangs heavy in the air.

I crash into the door frame when I come through the door. If Fargo's asleep, he's awake now. "Babe?" I say. I almost never call him that. "Fargo, are you here?"

I walk into the bedroom. He's not there. Then I see the closet door, slightly ajar. I go to look inside the closet. His things aren't inside—his shirts, his jeans. His suit jackets and slacks. His shoes are gone from the shoe hanger on the back of the closet door.

Did he finally do it? I expect to feel angry, but instead I feel relief. Relief washes over me. He's not going to be here in the morning, rushing around when I'm trying to fall back asleep before my 11 a.m. class. He's not going to be making coffee when I'm stumbling around, trying to get into the shower. He's not going to be using up all the hot water. He's not going to be in my way when I have to write my book and I want to stay up late and he wants to turn the light off. He's not going to want to have sex when I have a deadline. He's not going to be here. He's not going to be here at all.

I go to the kitchen and pour myself a glass of water. Nothing else seems to be missing. He didn't even take all of his clothes. I wonder when he'll come back for the rest of his things. The TV, that's his; he watches sports on it. He'll want that. I mentally divide up all of our assets. The couch is mine. The coffee table—his. The feeling of relief begins to ebb as the logistical nightmare of dividing our four years of life together starts to sink in.

And at the same time—who am I going to ask my questions to? Who am I going to cuddle with? Who am I going to bounce ideas off of, even when he has no idea what I'm talking about? Who's going to—Jesus, who's going to father my child? I sip my water, stumble toward the bed, kick off my shoes. I pull my phone out of my pocket, scroll down, find Fargo's number. My finger hovers over the button.

I can't do it. I can't call him, admit that I need him. That I need someone, someone to hold me when everything is spinning too quickly. And I know he needs me. He called me today because he still needs me.

And I need to be needed. I need to be desired by someone else. I need someone to want me. Fargo wants me. How does one feel close to another person?

I fall asleep in my teaching clothes, heavy with the knowledge that we're inexplicably tied together, no matter what we do. I want to tell Fargo this realization. But at the same time, I want to keep it to myself for just a little longer.

I wake up to an email from Steve: Everything all right? Thanks for coming out last night.

I ignore it. The last thing I want to do is talk to him. He's ruined himself for me. The idea that we could ever have a sexual relationship repulses me. He's my mentor, my most trusted confidant, and I would never ruin that relationship with something as cheap as sex. Sex is easy. You can do it with anyone. But emotional intimacy—that's difficult. How do you feel close to another person?

I have an email from Kenneth too: Good news. Can you meet for coffee?

I write him back right away, naming a cafe and a time. It's Saturday. He confirms, and I get dressed in normal clothes, jeans and a T-shirt. I shove my feet into sneakers. It feels good not having Fargo around. I'm enjoying my newfound freedom, even if it is short lived. I know that eventually I will have to call him, tell him I want him to come back. But not yet. I want to enjoy this time to myself just a little bit longer.

I walk to the cafe. It's nice out for once. It almost feels like spring. I'm wearing a light jacket. The winter is over, I think to myself. My birthday is coming up. Even the book doesn't feel so daunting. The shadow has lifted, somehow, overnight. Everything is going to be all right, I think as I push the door to the cafe open. Everything is going to be all right.

Kenneth is waiting at a table, coffee in hand. He has a grin on his face. "I got in," he says and wraps me in a completely inappropriate hug that I can't stop him from doing. "I fucking got it. Columbia. I got in, Caroline."

"That's incredible," I say. "Financial aid? Did they tell you yet?"

"Full ride." He beams. "Full goddamn ride. I'm going to Columbia. History master's degree. It's happening. They don't just give people full rides."

"I know that," I say. "I'm the one who told you that."

We sit down. He tells me about the fellowship he's won, about the teaching opportunities, about his plans for the future. "And I couldn't have done it without you," he says. "Seriously, I'm forever in your debt."

"Don't say that," I say. "You did the work. I just told them the truth about you."

He's grinning like a skull. I remember being that young, that happy. What happened? I guess—I guess I grew up. I have the sudden urge to email Steve, tell him—I don't know what. I don't know what. That he means the world to me. That he's my mentor, no matter what. But also that I can never cross that line with him. Because he means the world to me. Because he's important.

Kenneth is jabbering on, and I try to listen to him, but I can't make myself focus. "Professor?" he says. "Did you hear me?"

"What?" I say. "Yeah, I know, it sounds like a great opportunity."

My hand is on top of the table. He puts his hand on top of mine. Immediately my first instinct is to recoil, but his hand clamps down on mine, and I can't pull away.

"Thank you," he says. "I mean it. If there's anything I can do for you, let me know."

"Kenneth," I say.

"Anything," he says.

"Kenneth. Please."

"I just want you to know how much you mean to me," he says.

I give my hand a hard yank and pull it away. I take a sip from the coffee I've ordered to calm my nerves. My heart is beating in my chest. First Steve, now Kenneth. Am I emitting some kind of pheromone? "I understand that you're grateful, Kenneth, but this isn't appropriate."

"I don't care," he says. "I'm not going to be your student anymore in a couple of months. Then we could—"

"We aren't going to do anything," I say. "End of story."

"Oh," he says, and his face falls in the way that only twenty-one-year-olds who have just been rejected by their history professors can fall. "I see."

I stand up, pick up my coffee. "I'm going to go."

"Don't go," he says. "I want to celebrate."

"Celebrate with your friends."

"I thought you were," he says. "My friend."

"I'm your professor," I say. Then I gather my things and go.

My phone rings as I'm walking back. I no longer feel free and easy, like everything will be all right. I feel like a black cloud has come to ruin my perfect day. I don't know how I'm supposed to teach a class with Kenneth in it now. I don't know what I'm supposed to do at all.

It's Fargo. "Caroline?" he says. "Why didn't you call me? Didn't you get my note?"

"What note?" I say.

"The one that says I'm going on a team-building retreat with my job, and I'll be gone all weekend, and to call me when you woke up. Jesus. I was worried."

"Why didn't you just text me? Why did you leave me a note? This isn't the 1950s."

He sighs. "I don't know. It felt romantic. I left it on the fridge."

I get to our front door and open it. There is indeed a note on the fridge that says exactly what he says it does, but it says something else too: *I love you.* I don't mention this to him. I just say, "I see it," and then ask him how his day is going.

He tells me a little bit about the team-building retreat, which involves trust falls and those exercises where you have to get everyone over a rope in the woods, and I kind of tune him out while I make myself a bowl of soup. It feels good to listen to his voice. Then he asks me how my day has been, and I have to tell him, well, I've had a crazy twenty-four hours. I'll tell you about it when you get back, I say.

"You are coming back, right?"

"Why, do you miss me already?" he says.

"Something like that."

I can hear him smile over the phone. "When I get back," he says, "we should talk."

"I know."

"What do you want to talk about?"

"You're the one who said we needed to talk."

"Look, I don't want to fight with you."

"I don't want to fight either."

He pauses. "I have to go," he says. "Some of the guys want to go fishing, and I'm supposed to show them how to put a worm on a hook."

"Gross."

"Yeah, it'll be a good time," he says.

There's that beat where both of us are supposed to say, "I love you." Fuck it, I think to myself.

"I love you," I say.

"I love you too," he says.

Suspended Animation

I visit every August. Upstate. I don't mind the drive, the highways stretched out ahead of me like a million years, dodging small animals, driving through the night. I can do it in a day if I really push myself. Lately, I am older, and it's more difficult than it used to be. More difficult to pull over in a parking lot and take a cat nap. I wake up, and my shoulders are stiff, and Jonathan isn't there to rub them. "Why don't you fly up?" he asks me. "They would pay for it."

It's not about the money. I have the money. I like the drive, the feeling of the car underneath my feet. He wouldn't get it. The drive gives me time to think, time to figure out what I'm going to say. There's more than one way to say "I'm sorry." It's been six years, and I've come up with six new ways, and every year I come up with a new way, and every year it gets harder.

Driving, listening to the radio. I stop at a gas station and call Tommy. "You're the only one who still calls me that," he says when he picks up the phone. "You and Mike."

"We're your oldest friends," I tell him. "Well, I'm your oldest friend."

We go over the details—where I'm going to stay, when I should come over. Dinner would be best, we agree. That's what we've always done. Dinner with the whole family, Mike, the parents. Later Mike and I can have one-on-one time. I'm staying at a Holiday Inn not far from the house. They built it since I was last in town. I don't know what to expect. I've always liked hotels—the anonymity, the clean sheets and turn-down service. I'm looking forward to the swimming pool and room service and complimentary breakfast.

"Justine," Tommy says when we're done talking shop. "I'm glad you're coming."

"Tommy," I say. "I'll always come."

I hang up and go into the gas station to buy a pack of cigarettes. I haven't had a cigarette in a year, since the last time I made this drive. Jonathan would kill me if he knew I was smoking, but I know that sometimes he gets drunk with his buddies and buys a pack of menthols, the hypocrite. He thinks I can't smell it on him because of all the cologne and scotch. I don't say anything because if that's the only thing he's lying about, well, I'm not too worried, but still. I buy the cigarettes and a pink plastic Bic and thank the cashier.

He doesn't ask for ID. I'm thirty-one, but part of me still expects to get busted every time I try to buy smokes. Old habits, I guess.

"Have a nice day, ma'am," he says. I don't know when I became a ma'am. I'm still wearing the clothes I wore to work—burgundy suit, black heels. The cashier is probably nineteen.

"Right," I say. I drag my suitcase into the gas station bathroom and change clothes: jeans, T-shirt. Anything to make me look younger. I take my hair out of its clip and let it fall around my face. Mike always liked my hair down anyway. That's what he always said. I know I should call Jonathan, tell him I'm on the road, but part of me doesn't want to hear his voice just now. He doesn't like that I still make this trip, although he understands that I have to. He understands guilt.

I decide I'll call him when I stop to pee in another two hours and get back on the road. It's late, and there's almost no traffic. I lean back in my seat, driving with my elbows, smoking out the window. The car is a rental, and I know they'll charge me for smoking, but I don't care. This is part of the ritual. I'll drive through the night, stopping every few hours to get another cup of coffee and use the bathroom, and in the morning, I'll be there. The nice thing about Upstate is that it never changes. You leave and you get older, and then you come back and everything is just as you left it. Mike will be just the same, sitting in his same chair on the porch, smoking his Marlboros, yelling at the cat.

I fiddle with the radio. You'd think I'd be more worried about getting into an accident, driving at night, but I don't believe that lightning can strike the same place twice. I think I've reached my lifetime quota of car accidents. I've explained this theory to Jonathan, who thinks I'm crazy, but Jonathan thought I was crazy to begin with. I wouldn't ever bring up this theory to Mike.

Broken glass. Screaming. Blood like ropes. Whose blood? Not mine. Mike, where's Mike? Smell of smoke.

*

The road at night is comforting. Living in New York, you don't ever get to drive anywhere. I complain about it to Jonathan. I try to persuade him to rent a car with me, drive somewhere. He works weekends, doesn't want to take the time off work. He's a carpenter, builds stages, display cases. He makes a lot of money but isn't showy about it. He had his own apartment when we met, a queen-sized bed, air-conditioning. I was twenty-eight, not young enough to be a novelty, not old enough to be desperate. He's forty-two, eleven years older than I am. He doesn't want kids. That's one of the reasons I love him so much. Now we live together in a one-bedroom on Bushwick Avenue.

I guess you could say I'm happy. I don't want to tell that to Mike on the phone. We talk on Sunday nights. I want to tell him that I miss him, which is true, and that I'm lost without him, which is not. I have everything I want. I've had everything I want at other times in my life, and I know how easily it can all be taken away. I try not to take anything for granted. That's part of the reason I make these visits. To remember.

I've smoked too many cigarettes, and I'm starting to make myself sick. The sun is starting to come up, turning the sky a sickly pink. The GPS says I have another hour on the road.

I turn off of the highway, take side streets. Things are starting to look familiar. This is where I grew up. For a second, I imagine my mother is still alive, and I want to turn to her and say, "Wow, the neighborhood has really gone to shit, hasn't it?" but she's been dead two years, and there's no one for me to turn to. I pull off at a Wawa and call Jonathan, who I know will be awake. He's an early riser, one of the things I hate about him. He gets up and makes drawings for his job, pencil in his mouth, while I'm still sleeping, and then I roll over in our too big bed and wonder where he's gone and what if I have bad dreams?

"I'm right here," he'll call from the living room where he's got his drafting table set up by the window.

"Hey," he says when he answers. He sounds nervous, and I know he hates when I'm away, even if he'll never say it. "Are you driving safe?"

"No, I've stopped using turn signals altogether, and I'm going fifty over the speed limit," I say. I'm nervous too. It's hitting me all at once.

"Very funny," he says. I listen to him breathe. "Are you almost there? The way you drive, you should be almost there."

"I'm almost there," I say. "Another forty-five minutes, I think. Then I'll get to the hotel and probably sleep all day. Dinner tonight."

"Dinner tonight," he echoes. "Well. Give everyone my love."

"Right," I say, although I won't. I don't mention Jonathan at Mike and Tommy's house, the way you don't mention politics at Thanksgiving. "I'll talk to you soon. Love you."

"Uh-huh," he says. Jonathan has problems with "I love you." I know he means it, even if he doesn't say it, and that's good enough for me. "Talk soon."

The line goes dead. I wipe my sweaty palms on my jeans, get back in the car.

*

Sirens flashing. EMTs—at least I think they're EMTs. Rough hands pushing me around. Strapping me down. "Hang on, honey," someone says. "You're going to be okay."

"I am okay," I say. My voice sounds like it's coming from underwater.

"Shhh," the same someone says. "Don't try to talk. Just rest."

I do what they say.

Although I have not told Jonathan this, I bought a new dress for dinner. It doesn't fit as well as it did in the store, pinches my shoulders. Tommy opens the door. "You look great," he says. He always says that. Tommy is in love with me, which is unfortunate, given our history.

I've known Tommy since we were both fourteen and Mike was sixteen. We rode the school bus together. Tommy was this awkward kid with beautiful blue eyes who could rap all of Eminem. We used to walk to the park after school and lie in the grass. He talked about how he was always living in the shadow of his older brother, who was a lacrosse player, two years older, handsome. I talked about how I wanted to move to New York City.

I liked Tommy. I thought he was funny, and I thought his eyes were something else. I was also fourteen. I didn't know anything. When he invited me over to his house for dinner, I said sure. That was where the trouble started.

Mike was at dinner. He was preoccupied, talking about some lacrosse game, smelling like cigarette smoke. His mother yelled at him for a bad grade he had gotten on a physics test.

After dinner, Mike asked Tommy and I if we wanted to go outside and smoke a joint. Tommy said no. He didn't like weed. Tommy was going to grow up to be a doctor or a lawyer, just like his parents wanted. I said, why not? I had smoked before, but never with a cute junior, who was a lacrosse player to boot. What would my friends say?

We sat on the back porch, and Mike lit the joint. He asked me what my name was again, and I told him. He asked me if I had a boyfriend. I said no. He asked if his brother was my boyfriend. I laughed.

"Absolutely not," I said.

"Why not?" Mike said.

"I don't know," I said. "He's never asked me."

"Tommy's too chickenshit to ask you," Mike said.

"Do you have a girlfriend?" I asked.

Mike looked at me. He really looked at me. I think he hadn't thought anything of me before that. I was just some freshman his brother had brought home. But suddenly he saw me. "No," he said. "I don't."

He passed me the joint. Our fingers touched. His hand uncoiled, like a snake. He grabbed my wrist.

"What are you doing?" I said.

He jumped, as if coming out of a trance. "Nothing," he said. "Never mind."

After that, Mike and I were best friends, and Tommy was an afterthought. Sometimes the three of us hung out together, drinking lukewarm beer in their parents' basement, but mostly it was Mike and me. Mike and me roaming around the mall until close. Mike and me going to parties, him holding my hand in front of the cheerleaders and sneering at them when they tried to say something to me. Like all great love affairs, it felt unique, but really it wasn't. It was a lot of fumbling in the back seats of cars, a lot of peach schnapps stolen from parents' liquor cabinets, a lot of pleading and cajoling and begging and waiting for mothers to come home from work.

I never said anything to Tommy about what happened that night, although I guess nothing really happened, nothing that could be put into words. I started out as Tommy's friend, and I became Mike's girlfriend. It just happened, the way you just get a cold. I should have apologized, and I wanted to apologize, but I never did apologize, and then it was too late, and Tommy had other friends, and we didn't hang out anymore.

All of this seems like such a long time ago now that it feels funny to think about.

Tommy looks the same, only older. He is four months younger than me, I remember. He's a lawyer, just like he always said he would be. Works in Albany. He's divorced. Has a little bit of a paunch, maybe from drinking.

"How was the drive?" he asks, ushering me inside. "Everyone's in the living room."

"Fine, thanks." I follow him in. Brenda, their mother, is sitting on the couch. She's in her seventies but looks sixty. Still does Pilates every morning. Their dad, Daniel, is in his armchair. He's a retired neurosurgeon. "Good to see everyone."

"Good to see you, too, honey," Brenda says.

Mike's wheelchair is pushed up to the end of the couch. I go and sit next to him. "Mikey," I say. I'm the only one who's allowed to call him that. "How are you?"

"How the hell do you think I am?" he asks, but there's laughter in his eyes. "I'm the same, Justine. I'm always the same."

"I'm glad to hear that."

He puts his hand out, and I take it automatically. He squeezes my fingers. He looks thin. I wonder if he's eating enough, but I don't want to bring it up. He's wearing a plaid flannel shirt I don't remember and a pair of blue jeans. I used to do all the shopping for him. After we got married, for years he only wore clothes that I picked out. I wonder who is picking out his clothes now. Brenda, probably.

"So, how have you been? How's the sedentary life going?" he asks me.

"I'm not so sedentary," I say.

"You spend your days looking at old books," he reminds me. "I'd call that pretty sedentary."

"I like old books," I say. "They're easier to understand than people, that's for sure."

Before I can make a joke about Mike's sedentary life, Brenda breaks in. "Are you still living in Brooklyn, honey?"

"Yeah," I say. "In Bushwick. I've been in my current apartment for about a year."

Tommy is standing awkwardly in the doorway. He's the one who orchestrates these evenings, does the shopping, cooking. I can tell he wants us to go into the dining room and see what he's made for us. "Should we eat?" I say.

"Yes," Tommy says gratefully. "Please."

We file into the dining room, dutiful little lemmings. The Saltz house is perfectly decorated and tasteful; it almost looks like it should be in a magazine. I feel strange sitting in these chairs, as if I'll sully them with my presence. Mike once told me that he used to move his mother's various knickknacks around, just to see if she'd notice. In the mornings, they'd always be magically back in their places, as if nothing had happened. The table is hardwood, and the salad bowl is designer.

"This looks great," I say.

"Thank you," Tommy says. "I've been slaving away in the kitchen, awaiting your imminent arrival."

"God, Tommy," Mike says, wheeling himself into an empty space at the table. "You're such a nerd."

We eat and make small talk, and for a second this could all be normal, a normal family having dinner together, except it's not and we're not, and I have to keep reminding myself of that. I do not live here, and Mike is not my husband anymore. I catch him looking at me from over his wine glass more than once. He's always looked at me like that, ever since we were kids. As if I have the answers, as if I know something he wants to know.

I want to tell him to stop, but I can't, not with everyone here. Two days, I remind myself. It's just a weekend.

Mike puts his hand on my knee underneath the table.

*

Whiteness. Hospital bed. "Have you been drinking, ma'am?" Morphine in a yellow tube. Gasping for breath. Mike, where's Mike? Someone tell me where Mike is.

Am I screaming? No one can tell.

After dinner, Tommy cleans up, and the parents go to bed. They've always liked me. They think I'm a good influence on Mike. I kept him out of trouble in high school. When he was in college at U Albany, he came home on weekends to see me instead of going out partying with his friends. They didn't think we got married too young. "When you know, you know," they said when we told them. My parents, on the other hand, asked me if I was pregnant.

"No," I said indignantly.

"Not yet," Mike said, rubbing my belly. I socked him in the eye, gave him a black eye.

We were twenty-one and twenty-three. I had just graduated college with my degree in English lit. It seems like such a long time ago. Maybe it is.

"Hey, space cadet," Mike says. "You wanna go outside and smoke a joint?"

"I don't really smoke pot these days," I say.

"God, you really are getting old," he says. "No one calls it pot anymore. Besides, the stuff I get is medicinal, and it's totally good shit. Come on."

Tommy looks at us dubiously as we head outside. "Don't worry," I tell him. "I can put him to bed. I still remember how."

Mike rolls his eyes. "I can put myself to bed," he says. "I'm a grown man."

"Mike," I say. "Don't."

Outside the air is sticky. The crickets are chirping. It's pitch-black out. I forgot how dark it gets in the suburbs, and how quiet. Mike is humming something under his breath, something I don't recognize. My dress is starting to be really uncomfortable. I light a cigarette, and Mike lights the joint. The familiar smell rises in the air.

I wait for whatever he's going to ask me. Every time I come here, he has questions. Sometimes they're innocuous—do I remember what happened at a specific party several years ago? Sometimes they're more complicated. Once he asked me if I believed in soulmates.

When he doesn't say anything, I feel like I have to fill the silence. "I've had too much wine," I say.

"Are you trying to tell me that you're drunk?"

"I'm not drunk," I say defensively. "I can still drive. I'm just saying I shouldn't have had that third glass. Your father is very pushy."

"Yeah, he is," Mike says, smiling. Moths flock around the porch light. He exhales a long column of smoke and hands me the joint. I consider it and then take a hit. "Justine, I'm glad you came."

"Of course I came," I say. "I'll always come."

"You always say that," he says. "But someday, no, you won't."

"How do you know?"

"I just know," he says. "You're going to live your life. You're going to get married again, have babies. You won't have time to come see me. It'll be too painful."

"Mike," I say. "It's already too painful."

"That's not what I meant," he says. "I just mean, you're out there in the world, doing things, and I'm stuck here. Suspended animation. I can't exactly go out and meet girls, you know."

"You could. You could go online. You're a good-looking guy. I'm sure you could find someone."

"I've thought about it," he says. "I don't know. I don't know if I'm ready." He looks at me. "You're a tough act to follow."

"Don't." I take another hit of the joint, hand it back to him. Our pinkies touch. It was on this very porch, smoking a joint, that we first fell in love. The irony does not escape me. "You know I'm seeing someone, don't you?"

"Tommy told me," he says. "Some big shot in the city, right?"

"We're not going to get married," I say. "Ever. And we're not going to have babies. Honestly, I don't think I could—after. You know. So you don't have to worry about me moving on with anyone else. There are some things that you just don't move on from."

"That's good to know, I guess," he says. He presses the tip of the joint out on the edge of the porch and nods to me. "Can you help me inside? I want to go to bed."

"Sure."

His parents moved his room to the first floor after the accident. He says he's tired, so I wheel him down the hallway, wait while he uses the modified bathroom, and help him undress. He's right, he can do most of this himself. He needs my help to get out of the jeans, one leg at a time. I unlace his sneakers for him and put them in the closet.

When he's ready, I lift him into bed. I'm a little high, and I start to wonder how I'm going to drive back.

"Don't drive tonight," he says. "I don't want you getting into an accident. Sleep on the couch. Or sleep with me."

"I can't sleep with you," I say.

"Why not?"

"You know why not."

He pushes some hair out of his eyes. His hair is getting long again, like it was when I first met him. For a long time, he kept it short. I like it long.

"Just one night," he says. "You know, my dick still works. I'm still a man. I can still, you know, do things."

"Mike, I'm in a relationship."

"And that's the only reason?"

"No, that's not the only reason."

"Then what?"

"You know what."

He leans into the pillows, deflated. "Please," he says. That's all he says. Just "please."

I kick off my shoes. Unzip my dress, strip down to my bra and underwear. I peel back the covers and get into bed with him. His arms wrap around me. His legs lie uselessly against mine. I can feel his breath on my neck. I am almost certain that I won't sleep, so I don't even try. I just listen to the sound of his breathing, the rise and fall of his chest, until I don't know what time it is anymore, and then, I guess, I'm asleep.

The nurses come first. They don't tell me anything. The doctors come later. They only have bad news.

Concussion.

Broken ribs.

And the baby?

Silence.

I wake up to find Mike's arms wrapped around me like a vise. I untangle myself, get dressed, and let myself out before anyone else in the house knows I slept over. His parents like me, but I doubt they'd like me if they knew I was having sleepovers with their handicapped son. Tommy, especially. I get back to the hotel, take a long shower, and call Jonathan.

"How was the dinner?" he says.

"Bad," I say. "I slept over there. With Mike."

"Oh," Jonathan says. "Right."

"Nothing happened," I say. "I think he just didn't want to be alone. It's hard being cooped up in that house all the time. He feels like his life is over."

"Well," Jonathan says and then doesn't say anything for a long time. I know he's not angry, he wouldn't be angry like that, but I also know he's not happy with the situation.

"Look, I'll be home soon," I say. "Just hang on for another day or so."

"Okay," Jonathan says. "I will. For you."

"Thank you," I say.

I go downstairs and get something to eat from the hotel buffet, then take a long swim in the hotel pool and another shower. I'm supposed to meet Tommy for lunch at noon. I towel-dry my hair and get dressed, taking a moment to look at myself in the mirror.

I pull on a pair of slacks. It doesn't help to think about it. It's over, and nothing I can do will change it. On the drive to the bar where I'm meeting Tommy, I smoke three cigarettes in a row and feel ill.

I don't know what we're supposed to do for lunch because when I get there, it's really a bar and not a restaurant, but Tommy is already sitting at the bar with a burger in front of him, and he motions for me to sit down. "How are you?" he says. "I know this isn't easy for you."

"It's fine," I say. I don't want Tommy's sympathy. He was the best man at our wedding, and he was the first person I saw in the hospital after the accident. I remember it clearly—Tommy bursting into the hospital room, wild-eyed, smelling like bourbon. This was before he got divorced; he had been having an affair with another married woman. He only told me that because he thought I wouldn't remember, that I was too doped up on pain meds and dizzy with grief, but I remember.

At our wedding, he gave a toast. He said how much he loved the both of us and how happy he was that we were together. It was a lovely toast. I remember that too.

I order a beer and a burger with fries. Tommy's wearing a blazer and slacks even though it's the weekend. Like me, he's never fully off duty. He's always working. It's become a little habit of ours, to get lunch or something on these visits. Talk about the future. He knows his parents won't be around forever to take care of Mike, and then someone will have to do it. The hope, I guess, is that Mike stays pretty independent and can be moved to an apartment near either me or Tommy, and one of us can watch out for him. I don't want it to be me. I don't know how Jonathan would take that, being responsible for another person like that forever.

"I know you slept at our house last night," Tommy says. He's nursing an old-fashioned. "I saw your car in the driveway when I got up to pee."

"Nothing happened," I say. "I was just doing a favor for an old friend."

"And I get that," Tommy says. "But you can't get his hopes up like that. He still thinks that one of these days, you're just going to come home and everything is going to be all right. He still thinks the two of you are going to live happily ever after."

I have to admit, it took me a long time to stop believing that myself. "I'm sorry," I say. "I wasn't thinking."

"If you want to be with him, just do it," Tommy continues. "He's a good man, Justine. He really loves you."

"I know that."

"Then why?"

"It's complicated."

Those first few days in the hospital, when they told me that I had miscarried because of the accident and that Mike would never walk again, I wished I had died. I wanted to be with my baby. Mike was alive, everyone kept saying, I wasn't alone; but what they didn't understand was that our lives were completely different now. Nothing would ever be the same again.

"You just don't want to take care of him, do you?" Tommy says. "You can't deal with it. With the wheelchair."

"It's more complicated than that, Tom."

"No, it's not," Tommy says. He's got a slur to his speech that lets me know he's been sitting at the bar a while. "Look, I know you better than anyone, and I know that at the first sign of danger, you run for the hills. You don't want to be the chick with the wheelchair husband. You thought it would be too hard. So you bolted."

"You're being unfair," I say.

"Am I?" he says. "He's my brother. I have to take care of him, no matter what happens."

"He's my husband," I say. "I said 'til death do us part, and I meant it." I look down at my hands. "But something died in me that day. An important part of me. And I couldn't do it anymore."

"You could have had another baby," Tommy says.

"It's not about the fucking baby," I say.

"Then, what?"

"I don't know," I say. "I just—I realized that I couldn't do it." I put my head in my hands, thinking of how to verbalize something I've never been able to explain to anyone. My mother understood before she died. Sometimes you just can't. And you leave.

"Do what?"

"Be with him. When he was like that. Jesus, him in that fucking hospital bed, with all the tubes and the machines? And the wheelchair? And the bedpans? And needing someone to help him get in and out of bed every day? I know, I know, it could have been worse. But I didn't want to do it. I just didn't want to."

"A wife is supposed to be there for her husband." Tommy looks at me. "He loves you, Justine."

"Well, I'm not his wife anymore for a reason," I say.

Open road. Coming home from one of Mike's work parties. He was managing a supermarket chain, doing pretty well for himself. I was four months pregnant. Twenty-four years old. My parents thought we were crazy, having a baby in this economy. Mike kept rubbing my stomach. He was so excited, so happy to be a father, more so than any of my friend's husbands. It was a girl. It had been an accident, technically, but we hadn't been trying *not* to have a baby either. When it happens, it happens, we always said. We knew we wanted a big family. We were living in some awful condo downtown, but it didn't matter. There was room for a nursery, and Mike had just gotten a promotion at work. I was working at the local library, trying to keep off my feet.

The party had been good, lots of men shaking Mike's hand, lots of wives telling me how well I was carrying. Mike had had two glasses of wine but insisted he was fine to drive, and I was tired, so I let him. We had just celebrated our third wedding anniversary. We were that couple, the couple everyone wants to be, the couple everyone hates because they're so perfect. I have pictures of that time, Mike with his blond hair slicked back over his forehead, me with my stupid suburban mom haircut. We had both quit smoking.

The driver of the truck had been drunk. That's what the police said. Mike's blood alcohol was less than the legal limit, which was good for him. We won some money in the court case, but it all went to medical bills. I don't remember this part—this is what they told me later. We were at an intersection, and a truck ran a red light and smashed through the driver's side of our car at forty-five miles an hour. I flew through the windshield—the seatbelt had been hurting my pregnant belly, and I was only half-wearing it. Mike ended up crushed between the car door and the seat. It took EMS two hours to get him out, in which time his spinal cord was constricted. He broke several vertebrae.

They put us in the same hospital room, once we were both stable enough. We were close enough to hold hands. They told me my news first, then his. The baby. His legs. I thought I would die. I doubled over with grief. My mother was there, this was before she died, and she held me tightly and told me that everything would be all right.

I was in the hospital two weeks. Mike was there longer; they had to run tests, start him on physical therapy, teach him how to use the wheelchair. His parents made modifications to their home so he could live there. I was welcome, of course, but I had no intention of going back there. From my hospital bed, I applied to jobs in New York City. I couldn't look at Mike. I wasn't going to be the one to take care of him, now that he couldn't take care of himself. While he was still in the hospital, I went to our condo, packed up my things, and left.

I don't know why I did it. It seemed imperative at the time, the way you have to scratch an itch. The divorce papers would come much later. After a while, it was as if I had never been married at all.

Tommy is drunk when I lead him back to my hotel room. I don't know why I do this. I want to hurt him, but more than that, I want to hurt myself. I want the flagellation and the hair shirt. I want penance. This is my penance.

I undo his tie. "What are you doing, Justine?" he asks. He smells like bourbon, like he did the night of the accident. I think about what he said. "You're not a good person." Tommy isn't a good person either. He cheated on his wife. I've never cheated on anyone before. I suppose I'm about to cheat on Jonathan, but our relationship is more nuanced than that, and Jonathan will understand. He'll have to.

"I'm not doing anything," I say.

They're brothers, I tell myself. There's a certain physical resemblance. I've slept with Mike more times than I've slept with anybody else, and I know his body better than I know my own. The differences are what I notice. Tommy is stockier with a bit of a beer belly. He has more hair on his chest, and it runs down to his stomach. His hands are less sure of themselves. He waits for me to unbutton my blouse before putting his hands around my waist. He allows me to take off my own pants.

I want to turn on the TV, turn off the lights, do something to distract myself. There is nothing but the sound of his breathing, the bourbon taste of his mouth. We kiss briefly. A memory dislodges—Tommy, drunk at my wedding, finding me in the line for the restroom.

"A bride should never have to wait to take a piss on her own wedding day," he said. Then,something passed over his face. I thought he was going to throw up. "I love you, you know that?" he said.

"I know that," I said.

I wonder if he thinks about me. I don't think about him, not often. When I do, it's in conjunction to Mike or coupled with feelings of guilt. Somehow I don't think much will change. I let him fumble with the condom I purchased in the hotel lobby as I lie on my back, waiting for this to be over. I need Mike to know, for sure, that I'm not coming back. I need them both to know. This is the only way to be sure.

He pulls down his pants, hitches himself up, and pushes into me. It's awkward. I wonder when the last time he did this was. Probably a long time. I think of Jonathan, with the tattoo on his smooth chest, Jonathan's hands on my body, Jonathan's breath in my ear. I'm going to have to tell him what happened. God, I miss him.

We met at a bar near my old apartment. I had been in the city several years, dated some, but nothing had stuck. I was still heartbroken, I guess. Not really looking for anything. It's funny how that happens. Always when you least expect it.

He sat down next to me, knees knocking into mine. "Sorry," he said in a way that made me think he wasn't really sorry. He had a quiet confidence, knew the bartender. In those days he still smoked cigarettes—menthols. He was wearing a Carhartt jacket and black jeans. Clean-shaven.

"It's fine," I said. Then, feeling bold: "What are you drinking?"

"Whatever you're having," he said and then looked at the drink in front of me. "Jesus. Who drinks banana daiquiris on a Tuesday night?"

"I've had a bad week."

He signaled the bartender. "One banana daiquiri, please."

We slipped into each other's lives the way you put on a pair of gloves. Easy fit. I wanted to write a book: *This Is What Happens After You Marry Your High School Sweetheart.* Jonathan thought it was hilarious. He didn't believe in true love; he believed in seeing what happened next. He believed in late nights and early mornings and waffles and feeding the cat on time. He thought it was laughable that I had already met my soulmate and that it hadn't worked out.

"I don't believe in soulmates," he told me once.

"What do you believe in then?"

We were lying in bed, naked, tangled in the sheets. "I believe—" he broke off. "I believe in making the world a better place for the people you care about."

"Hey," Tommy says. "Are you still with me?"

Right. Tommy. I nod, my stomach lurching. "I'm here."

"Sorry, you seemed a little spaced out for a second. Are you sure, I mean, do you still want to do this?"

"Are you going to finish?"

He considers. "I don't think so," he says. "I'm too drunk."

It's barely two in the afternoon. The light is coming in through the blinds. "Let's just stop then. I'll drive you home."

He rolls off me, buttons up his pants. "You're not going to tell Mike about this, are you?"

"Of course I'm going to tell Mike about this," I say. I pull on my shirt, underwear, go to the bathroom, and pee with the door open. "Don't you think he should know?"

In the mirror, my face looks haggard. Old.

"I really don't think that's such a good idea."

"I don't believe in secrets, Tommy," I say.

Tommy's face has gone pale. He tucks his shirt in. "My brother will never speak to me again."

"You should have thought of that before you stuck your dick in me."

"You wanted me to," he says, indignant.

"Sure, whatever."

I put on a pair of sweatpants and slide my feet into my shoes. Tommy follows me to the elevator in silence. The drive to the Saltzes' house is short, and Tommy smokes like a chimney the whole ride. I don't have a stomach for cigarettes.

Mike is on the porch when we pull into the driveway.

Tommy is first to speak. "I'm sorry," he says. Mike looks at him. He's smoking a cigarette; the ember burns in between his first and second fingers.

"Come on," he says, looking tired. "Really? Justine? Did you really?"

I don't say anything. I don't even get out of the car.

"Mike, I'm sorry," Tommy starts again, halfway out of the car door.

"Don't," Mike says and wheels himself inside.

Tommy looks at me. "You did this," he says. "This is your fault."

I nod. "I know," I say. I look out the windshield at the house in front of me. The house where I've eaten dinner so many times, where I've slept. Where I've looked Mike's parents in the eye and told them I loved their son. "Tommy," I say. "Get out of the car."

"So you're just going to leave?" he asks.

"Yes," I say. "That's exactly what I'm going to do."

"And leave me to clean up your mess?"

"It's your mess too, Tommy."

He shuts the car door. "I can't believe you," he says. He walks into the house. I watch him disappear. Then I start the car. I drive away.

In the city, I lie with my head in Jonathan's lap. He plays with my hair. There's a movie on the TV, but neither of us is watching it.

"You're not sorry, are you?" he asks me.

I hate this, the way Jonathan has always been able to read me. "I am and I'm not. It's for the best. That I don't go up there anymore."

"It scares me," Jonathan says in a small voice. "That you could do something like that to someone you love. I don't know what you're capable of."

"I would never do anything to hurt you," I say. But even as I say it, I know in my heart that I could walk away from him too. I could walk away from anything. Because I've done it before. Because that's the kind of person I am.

"I know that," Jonathan says. "But what if it had been me in that car accident? You're telling me you wouldn't make those same choices again?"

"It's different," I say, sitting up. I look him in the eyes. "Jesus, it's different. I'm older. I was only a baby then. Twenty-four. I didn't know what I was doing."

"I want to believe you," he says. "But I don't."

"What are you saying?"

"I'm saying that I love you," he says slowly. This is a revelation. Jonathan has never said he loves me before. "But I don't trust you."

"We can't have a relationship if we don't have trust."

"I know that."

"So, what now?"

Jonathan exhales through his front teeth. "I'm saying," he says, "and I know you don't want to hear this, but I'm saying I think you need to make it right."

Jonathan and I stand in front of the Saltz house, holding hands, while I try to work up the courage to ring the doorbell. "Come on," Jonathan says. "You can do it." I want to tell him he has no idea what I can and can't do, but I can't make the words come out of my throat. We both agreed it would be better if he came with me, but now it just feels like worlds are colliding. This was his condition—that I make things right with Mike if he and I are to continue our relationship. I want to be with Jonathan more than I want anything else; I want to move forward. Mike has been holding me back for too many years. But I can't bring myself to ring the bell.

"Justine," Jonathan says, "you're being childish." He knows I hate when he makes fun of my age; the eleven years that separate us are a sore point to me. "Just ring the damn bell."

I look at Jonathan's face: beaky nose, gray-blue eyes, the most familiar face in the world. I raise my hand to press the button. As I do, the door swings open. There's Mike, already waiting.

"You've been standing on the porch for fifteen minutes," he says. "You gonna come in or what?"

He rolls into the living room. One of his old jokes is that he never needs to look for a place to sit down. I sit on the couch; Jonathan takes an armchair. "Do you want anything?" Mike says. "We probably have some beers in the fridge."

"Mike, you don't have to—"

"It's fine."

He doesn't exactly seem happy to see me, but he doesn't seem like he's going to bite my head off either, so I settle down on the couch. "Why are you here?" he asks me. "I pretty much assumed I was never going to see you again."

"Well, Jonathan—" I break off. "This is Jonathan. Jonathan, this is Mike. Jonathan thought I should make things right with you."

"Right. So you didn't care, but your boyfriend felt guilty that you fucked me over."

"Mike." I am surprised at how much venom is in his voice. "It's not like that at all. Of course I feel bad about everything. You know that. I just didn't know what to do."

"Don't bother explaining," he says. "You've always been shallow, Justine. Shallow and weak. Always more concerned with taking the easy way out. I understand everything. Things got too hard, and you left. You should be warned, man," he says, looking at Jonathan, "that the second the going gets tough, Justine here gets going. Whenever we would fight, she would always walk out on me."

"Mike, you're not being fair. We were both under a lot of pressure."

"What kind of pressure were you under?' he says, suddenly yelling. "My fucking legs don't work!"

It's like all the air goes out of the room. I realize we've never had this conversation, not in all the years. It's always been about how we still love each other, how we can't be together, how I can't deal with his disability. We've never talked about what we've lost. Jonathan is pasty white. I can tell he doesn't want to be here. But I'm already crying. It's too late. We've crossed the line.

"I lost a baby," I say quietly. "I lost my baby. You don't know what it feels like to have something growing inside of you and have it suddenly be gone."

"Look," Jonathan says, "I don't think it's productive to argue about who suffered more."

Mike sneers. "Oh, Mister Boyfriend is going to play peacemaker now, is he?"

"Mike, don't be cruel."

"I'll be whatever I want to be," Mike says. "You did what you were going to do, Justine. I know what kind of person you are, and that's that. I loved you. I really did."

"And I loved you," I say. "I just couldn't do it. I'm sorry for that. I needed to get away."

"Well, good for you," he says. "Because you did."

Jonathan stands up. "I think we should go."

I stand up too. "Mike, I really am sorry."

"I'm sorry too," he says, and it's like all the air has gone out of a balloon.

We leave.

On the drive back, we don't talk for the first few hours. There's nothing to say. I keep thinking of Mike in that chair, shutting the door behind us, going back to whatever it is he does in the days alone, watching TV, playing video games, talking to girls on the internet. Puttering around the house. I can't stop thinking about how stuck he is, how trapped, how it's my fault. If we were still married, I could have done something for him, helped him stay motivated, something. I feel guilty, more guilty than I've ever felt. After a few hours of me staring out the window, Jonathan turns down the radio and says, "Stop beating yourself up."

"I can't stop."

"You did a shitty thing, you apologized, and it's over." Jonathan reaches into the glove box and hands me my cigarettes. "Here. I won't say anything if you smoke in the car."

"Thank you."

I light one, and he wrinkles his nose but doesn't complain. "It's really over, isn't it?"

"You suffered a loss. You talked it out. I don't know if you'll ever be over it, but it's over."

"I guess you're right."

I look out at the lights of New York City, coming up ahead of us in the windshield. The buildings shine brighter than the stars. I don't feel particularly hopeful. But with Jonathan besides me, smoke in my mouth, Mike behind me, I feel almost okay. Almost all right. Maybe that's the best I can ask for. Maybe that's all we get.

About the Author

Joanna Acevedo is a writer living and working in New York City. She is the author of the poetry collection *The Pathophysiology of Longing* (Black Centipede Press, 2020) and received her BA in Literary Studies from the New School in 2019. She is a Hospitalfield 2020 Interdisciplinary resident, NYU Goldwater Fellow, prose editor at *Inklette Magazine*, and is currently an MFA candidate at New York University. In her spare time, she teaches creative writing, pursues the cheapest beer+shot combo deals, and spends time with her cat. She is working on her debut novel.

Acknowledgments

Thank you to the following people, without whom this book would not have made it out of my computer and into the world.

To my wonderful parents, Anne Finkelstein and James Acevedo, for listening to me talk on and on about books and writing, for raising me, for everything in between.

To Anna Kampfe for being a lovely friend and letting me be the only Aries in her life, a title I shall wear with pride.

To Nora Goodbody for being a great friend and more important, a first reader, for always telling me to keep writing, for always being down to cry when I've written something new.

To Brady Flanigan, well, you know why.

To Joshua Furst, for incredible mentorship and support over the years. I wouldn't be where I am today, the person I am today, without you.

To my teachers at NYU: Katie Kitamura, John Freeman, Jeffrey Eugenides, you have taught me so much.

To my fellow students at the Creative Writer's House 2019–2021, you inspire me every day, and I am blessed to know all of you.

Thank you to the baristas at Variety Coffee Roasters on Wyckoff and Himrod, for always being there to pour me an iced latte when I needed an extra push to write that new ending, that new bridge, that new story. I couldn't have done it without you. Especially you, Matt, wherever you are.

Lastly, to any one of my friends who read this book in its infancy, who gave me feedback and notes before it was published. I cannot thank you enough.

www.ingramcontent.com/pod-product-compliance
Lightning Source LLC
Chambersburg PA
CBHW070648100726
47907CB00007B/2143

* 9 7 8 1 7 3 6 4 0 3 3 0 3 *